D1739021

Kickin' Up Dust

Operation Cowboy Book 1

All Rights Reserved

Copyright Em Petrova 2017

Print Edition

Electronic book publication April 2017

This Marine follows the rules. This cowgirl is all about breaking them.

Operation Cowboy, Book 1

After losing his best friend and CO, Matt, in combat, Brodie Bell didn't think his spirits could sink any lower. He was wrong. One look at his and Matt's storm-flattened hometown nearly levels him.

Los Vista needs a leader, and as Brodie takes the weight of the world on his shoulders, he comes up with a plan. Merge the two ranches left standing, pray for a good calving season…and keep his hands too busy to *get* busy with Matt's sexy little sister.

Danica was in pigtails when Brodie and Matt went off chasing glory. Now she's a woman with a broken heart, but if Matt knew of the depraved cravings Brodie ignites in her body, he'd haunt her from the grave.

As they work to mend miles of broken fences, Brodie fights to ignore Danica's tiny cutoff shorts and mile-long legs—and to ignore the "weapon" that's locked and loaded in his

Levis. Because the last thing he wants is to dishonor his friend's memory by ravishing the sweetest little cowgirl he's ever laid eyes on.

Warning: Involves a sweet and sassy ranch girl who knows her way around a rope, and a Marine turned cowboy who'd like to tie her down and spank her until she begs for more.

Dedication

To the men and women who serve our country and give up so much so we may have freedom. Thank you all.

Other books in this series:
SPURS   'N   SURRENDER

Kickin' Up Dust

by

Em Petrova

Chapter One

"First thing I'm going to do is hug my momma and ask if she's made any biscuits." Brodie rubbed a hand over his stomach, sliding his Marine Corps T-shirt over his hard abs. "My gut's been growling for three tours."

In his early years as a Marine, he'd dreamt of Momma's light, fluffy biscuits going down with homemade peach jam. It was one of the only things from his past that hadn't faded. He couldn't quite remember how his momma's face looked, but he did recall the stern lines between his father's brows. He'd seen those twin creases enough growing up. They were etched into his brain.

"I haven't been dreaming about biscuits for three tours," Wydell drawled.

1

"He's been dreamin' about your momma," Garrett quipped.

"You should hear how loud he is," Boyd added.

The laughter of his three childhood buddies filled the car. They'd crawled alongside him in the desert sands of Afghanistan, and then through two more tours in Iraq. But the car had a hole where Matt would have sat.

While they fired off more jokes about who was noisiest in his bunk, Brodie stared at the gray ribbon of road stretching ahead. All four windows of the old Ford were rolled down, and he dragged in a huge breath of Texas air. Home was near. He could smell it.

Garrett, in shotgun, nudged Brodie with his elbow. "The old Ford's gotten us here."

"Yeah, she's done well." Brodie swiped his fingers through the dust on the dashboard. The plastic was cracked after being baked in the Texas sun for the past eighteen years. Yeah, she was nothing to look at but would get them to the end of the line—Los Vista, Texas. And on their pooled budget of $998.

As astute as always, Garrett picked up on Brodie's mood. Brodie forced a smile. He felt his eyes crinkle with it, but his chest was devoid of happiness. "I don't know why they're talking about my momma. It's yours we all dreamed of as teens."

Garrett groaned. "God, don't talk about my mother."

Brodie laughed, this time for real. They'd all discussed Mrs. Gentry's toned figure enough times to know Garrett didn't appreciate it. Eventually he'd taken to tackling whoever mentioned her tits.

Brodie's amusement faded as they passed a road sign for a town just outside of Los Vista. His homecoming was darkened by what he was bringing back with him—the belongings of one Sergeant Matt Pope. Best friend, platoon leader.

The familiar knot clogged Brodie's throat at the thought of all the townsfolk who'd waved them off with a parade years ago. He'd only returned as often as he could in the first year or two, but Matt had come more often to see his family between tours of duty.

Now Matt wouldn't come back at all, and Brodie was the most logical person to deliver the folded flag and dog tags to his family.

"Damn," he murmured, but nobody heard. The wind carried his curse away, though the whole car seemed to take on Brodie's state of mind. In the back, the guys settled. Garrett looked out his window.

Even the enormous Texas sky seemed too low right then. It didn't leave Brodie a lot of breathing room, and his chest started to burn.

He counted to fifty. Then backward. By fives and tens. His method of dealing with panic attacks hardly worked, but at least it distracted him for the last twenty miles of their drive.

By the time they reached the county line, his anxiety transformed to a lurch of excitement. *Home.* Miles of fields dotted with cattle. The familiar gates of the ranch that had been in his family for two generations.

Garrett leaned forward and moved his face closer to the windshield. "Where the hell is it? We shoulda been passing DeLoe's Farm Supply by now."

Brodie swung his head left and right, searching for landmarks, but the sides of the road were empty, save for some paved lots.

Then he saw it—a wooden structure caved in on itself. He blinked as he drove past, and the guys stretched their necks to see too.

"What the fuck was that?" Brodie asked.

"I think it was…Marley's Insurance office?"

"Nah, couldn't be. It's up the road a ways." Brodie strained to see farther ahead. Strange how the road was empty too. They hadn't passed a single car coming out of Los Vista. Their hometown wasn't exactly big, but it was always busy. There wasn't a lazy or idle person in Los Vista.

"No, man, I saw the sign," Garrett said.

Brodie threw a look in the side mirror but couldn't make out what Garrett meant. All he saw was a heap of fallen wood.

Realization slammed him smack in the forehead. The place was just...gone. "Holy. Fuck." The words came out of Brodie like a prayer—a prayer for him to be hallucinating. Surely what he was seeing wasn't real.

Their town—leveled. The school a jumble of bricks and glass. Cars twisted and upside down. Trees snapped off like toothpicks. The few restaurants in ruins.

Beyond that, nothing. He couldn't see a barn or silo for miles.

"Jesus Christ, what happened?" he breathed. He'd been in range of a couple grenade blasts during his time as a Marine, and the concussions had rattled him though they had done no damage. He felt the same way now—as if he'd been thrown by a blast.

"It's fucking gone. The town's gone. Either there was a war here or a tornado."

"But…nobody said anything to me. My parents didn't say anything about a tornado," Garrett said.

Brodie slowed the car and stopped in the middle of the road. There was no risk—they were totally alone.

For long seconds, nobody spoke. He had a crawling sensation that he was back in combat, looking at the devastation their team had wrought. But no, this was definitely natural. The trees weren't lopped off from bombs. They were snapped and twisted from high winds.

"Where the fuck's my barn?" Garrett's voice raised as he thrust a finger toward the place his ranch should be in the distance. "It should be there."

Brodie exchanged a glance with him and then stomped on the gas. As they thundered up the road at eighty miles an hour, he had a distinct feeling of being in an apocalypse movie. The wild birds of panic flapped in his chest again, but no amount of counting would distract him this time.

* * * * *

"Garrett's family's living in a lean-to on their property. Their cattle are all gone with the rest of the ranch." Brodie's father eyed him from the head of the table. Between them were roast beef, mashed potatoes, corn, and those light, fluffy biscuits he'd been dreaming of.

But now they were untouched.

Brodie shook his head. "How'd the tornado miss us?"

His momma lifted a shoulder in a depressed shrug. Guilt reflected in her deep brown eyes. Their four walls were still standing, if a little battered. They hadn't lost many head of cattle, while their neighbors and friends had lost everything. Momma had survivor's guilt.

Boy, did he know all about that.

"The only other property that didn't take a big hit is the Pope Ranch."

Brodie's head snapped up at his father's words. Suddenly, there was no way he could eat those biscuits or anything else on the table.

He felt himself nod. "That's good. They've...lost enough."

Of course the family had been informed of Matt's death. They hadn't traveled to Arlington Cemetery to see him buried, which was how Brodie came to possess the flag that had covered his coffin. The coffin he and his buddies had carried.

He shook himself and snagged a biscuit. The sooner he visited the Popes, the better. Then he could let his past go, stop being a Marine and start being a cowboy. They all shared this dream, but it looked as though his friends would have a harder time, seeing how they no longer had ranches.

"And the people just lost heart," Momma said, pushing the crock of jam in his direction.

"They left?"

"Almost all moved to surrounding towns."

"But the ranches…their land. How can they just leave it?"

"Many are taking insurance payouts and putting their acreage up for sale. Rebuilding is a huge undertaking. Many aren't up to the challenge. The Popes still have their place, though." His pa forked potatoes into his mouth.

What a fucked-up mess. Coming home to find they didn't have a town? And only Brodie had a home—the other guys were camping out in Garrett's family lean-to.

"How much cattle you running?" Brodie looked at his father. Now that he was back, he realized his memories of his pa's face weren't really perfect. Either that or his father had changed. Aged.

Hell, I have too. What were his parents seeing on his face? Lines from squinting into a scope all day, waiting to snipe some general before their whole platoon was killed. Brodie's skin had been tanned to leather, and he bore a jagged scar down the side of his face.

But all these changes might have taken place if he'd stayed in Los Vista and cowboy'd. The lines and tan naturally occurring from the sun, the scar from being kicked by a bull. It happened.

"Just a hundred." His father said the word like *hunnerd.*

Brodie gaped. A hundred head of cattle? Back in the day, they ran triple that. "I guess that means you don't have any ranch hands."

"Nope. And the bulls? Gone. I had them separated in the west pasture when the storm came through."

Shhhit. No bulls? What kind of ranch survived without bulls? And why hadn't Pa bought more at auction?

"Times have changed, son. The money's stretched so thin we can't rescue the ranch. We're clinging on here. Don't rightly know for how long."

Brodie set his fork and knife down with a clatter and stared between his parents. "Are you thinking about pulling out too?"

Momma reached across the table and rested a hand on his forearm. The touch felt foreign as hell—when was the last time he'd had a woman's touch, even his mother's?

"It's hard, honey. We never realized how much support we had from the neighbors. And your pa and I aren't getting any younger. We can't use what little savings we have to buy more cattle."

"What about calves? It's time to breed so we have calves." Brodie's appetite was gone, even though he stared longingly at his plate.

The home-cooked meal should have topped off a wonderful homecoming. But he still had to visit the Popes.

His father polished off a biscuit. "I don't see us having any calves, Brodie."

"Shit." He pushed away from the table.

"Brodie, where are you going?" His mother's voice pitched higher as he strode from the kitchen.

"Over to the Popes'. I'll be back by dark." He grabbed the paper bag and headed out on foot. Garrett and the other guys had the car because Boyd and Wydell had tracked down their parents to the neighboring town. Tomorrow they'd drive over and have their reunion. Brodie didn't mind walking. Besides, the Popes' place bordered theirs.

Tall grasses swished against his legs as he crossed the field. It was high time to make hay. Why hadn't his pa cut it at least? And surely there was a guy or two left in Los Vista to hire for a couple days' work.

As he crested the hill and set eyes on the Popes' ranch house, a knife of regret sliced through his chest. He issued a ragged breath and fought the memory of Matt's final moments. Cradled in Brodie's arms, blood trickling from his mouth.

Take care of yourself, Pup. Those were his last words before his eyes had glazed over and he'd stared sightlessly at the sky. The wrong sky — not a Texas sky.

They were all supposed to grow old together, get together once a week for poker games and to shoot the shit. But Matt had bugged out early, and now it was up to Brodie to hold the group together.

Only they couldn't possibly all stay in Los Vista. Not without a miracle.

A dog barked, and he searched the land for a glimpse of the animal. When he saw the black hound bounce above the grasses, ears flopping, Brodie's heart lurched. His eyes blurred as a total sense of joy overcame him.

The dog rushed him. Hit him square in the chest with his enormous paws, rocking Brodie back. He laughed and hooked the dog around the neck. "Hey, Crow. How are ya, boy?"

Crow wagged not only his tail but his whole body. He snaked his pink tongue out and licked Brodie's nose.

It had been Matt's idea to name the stray puppy Crow, partly because of its coloring and partly because they'd found him near the ruins. On the outskirts of town, a cave was hidden in the land, but most of the residents of Los Vista knew about it and had visited it at some point. The guys had taken plenty of girls there, knowing they'd be spooked enough to want the boys' arms around them.

Nobody knew what Indian tribe had inhabited the cave, but there were plenty of drawings and some artifacts. The dog had been found near enough the cave that Matt had called it an Indian pup, and it had become Old Crow. Just Crow for short.

He patted the dog on the back and it dropped to all fours. Together they walked the rest of the way to the long ranch house. Each step felt weightier. Crow stopped wagging his tail and paced slowly alongside him.

The house was unchanged, bar a few shingles that had been torn off the roof during the storm. Of course, the miles of fence running between properties was ripped up or the posts were slanted.

Brodie stepped onto the low, wooden porch. Here they'd played cowboys and Indians as boys. They'd sat on the steps and had their first stolen sips of beer.

When he pulled open the screen door, it still gave a pleasant creak. He rapped on the familiar wood while Crow panted at his side. He tried not to think of his reason for being there or what he was going to say. There were no words for this occasion. He'd do what he'd always done in times like this — he'd wing it.

Footsteps sounded inside, and his heart began to race. The throb spread until his temples ached and his eyeballs felt as if they were bulging.

Fifty, forty-nine, forty-eight…

The door opened, and he found himself staring at slim bare feet with red painted toenails. He followed them up to narrow ankles, curvy calves, thighs the warm, smooth color of a brown egg. He let his gaze rush the rest of the way up to the woman's face.

His jaw dropped.

Her full, ripe lips fell open.

For a heartbeat, he couldn't think of who this gorgeous, tawny creature was. Long, dark hair that spilled over rounded breasts. Her eyes the same color as—

"Pup!" She launched herself at Brodie, climbing him like a tree.

On reflex, he locked his arms around her and held her to him, his panic forgotten, a low ache spinning through his gut. His cock twitched at the feel of her crotch against his fly, warm and covered only by a thin strip of denim and some cotton panties. At least that's what fantasy played in his head.

"Danica?" he choked out, catching a whiff of her hair that left him with a strangely familiar feeling. She smelled of hayfields and bonfires. Of sour apples and everything he'd loved about spending time with the Popes.

"Jesus Christ, Brodie. Oh dear God." She wrapped her arms and legs around him, unwilling to let go.

He held her effortlessly, though Matt's kid sister was nearly as tall as he was. Flat-footed she must have reached six feet. "Holy fuck, Danica." He buried his face against her hair and just breathed. If driving into Los Vista had left him feeling empty, holding Danica felt like coming home.

She pulled back to look into his eyes. The cornflower depths of hers were filled with tears, and while her smile was wide and her teeth blindingly white, he saw the glint of pain in her eyes.

Very gently, he set her on her feet. She stood before him, tall and curvy. A real cowgirl in a plaid top rolled to the elbows and knotted at the waist, affording him a glimpse of tanned midriff.

Fucking hell, she wore a silver hoop in her bellybutton.

He snapped his gaze back to her face in time to see her features crumple.

"Oh sweetie." He reeled her into his arms again, just holding her and swaying back and forth as her grief crowded out the feelings of happiness they'd shared. The bag he still held seemed to weigh a hundred pounds, and he kept his wrist cocked so the bag didn't touch her back. He wasn't ready for her to ask what was inside. Right now, he just wanted to hold her.

"When did you get in?" she sniffled.

"Few hours ago."

"And…" Her breath washed over his neck, raising hairs he didn't realize he had there.

"And the town's a fucking mess."

"Nobody told you?"

He shook his head. When she withdrew from his hold to meet his stare, she'd composed herself a little. No tears wet her cheeks though some lingered in her eyes. She waved at the porch furniture, and he nodded.

Her tanned bare feet made scuffing noises as she crossed the porch, and she tucked them under her as she sat in an old wooden chair with a cushion. Brodie purposely skirted a certain chair and sank into another. One that didn't hold so many memories of the man — or boy, rather — who used to sit there.

Brodie's throat clogged again. He set the bag on the floor between his feet, leaned his elbows on his knees, and dropped his head into his hands. *Forty-seven, forty-six, forty-five.*

A whispery touch on his arm made him look up into those tear-bright eyes that were breaking his goddamn heart. "I'm glad you're home, Pup. It's good to see you."

He reached for the bag, but she tightened her grip on his arm. Her fingers were long and slender, shaped so much like her brother's.

"I know what you brought, but I'm not ready to see it, okay? Let's just talk. Like old times. Please?"

He bobbed his head in agreement and sat back in his chair to look at the only thing left in Los Vista worth seeing. Matt's kid sister had certainly grown up.

* * * * *

Danica could almost feel her ovaries exploding as she drank in the image of Sergeant Brodie Bell. He must have packed on fifty pounds of solid muscle since going off to war with her brother. His arms were roped, his biceps bursting from his T-shirt sleeves. And mother of pearl, the way his jeans hung on his hips could make a girl go a little crazy.

Her nipples were two tight buds, and she feared he could see them distending her top, since she hadn't bothered with a bra after her shower. All day long the torture device had dug into her shoulders and chafed her sides. Someday maybe she'd fabricate and patent a bra made for cowgirls. One a girl could rope and ride in without discomfort.

She watched Brodie's face change as they stared at each other.

"You lost the braces."

Oh hell. Was that all he saw when he looked at her? That she no longer had buck teeth? In school they'd called her Easter, because someone said her teeth resembled the Easter Bunny's.

"Yeah, Pup. What of it?" She shot him a grin, quite aware of how perfect her problem area was now.

A ghost of a smile tipped the corner of his lips but he didn't let it reach his eyes. Those were the deepest brown, nearly black. Cool, calculating almost. She could easily see how battle and probably the latest events had changed him.

"That nickname can't rile me anymore. What do you think they called me in boot camp?" He extended his forearm, where a cute little black puppy was tattooed. Its jaws were wide open, and blood dripped off its fangs.

She noted the veins snaking over his arm and felt her nipples tighten further. What was the matter with her? This wasn't the time for lust or the person to lust over. Matt was dead, and Brodie had the horrifying job of delivering his belongings to her parents.

She swallowed hard and averted her gaze. Trying to think up anything to say that didn't have Matt's name in the sentence was making her edgy. "Can I get you something to drink?"

"Nah, just came from dinner."

"So the town—"

"Your ranch is—"

They spoke together, and she gave a low laugh. He nodded for her to continue. "The storms came a month back. Three twisters converged at the same time. Some had no warning at all."

"Casualties?" He spoke as if it were war. At the time it had felt that way.

A shiver prickled the hair on her forearms. "Two dead. The Macallums."

He blew out a long whistle. "Damn, that's harsh." They were an old couple everyone had adored. They'd taught school together, retired together, and perished together.

For a moment they were both silent as if in observance of their memory. Finally, Brodie looked up into her eyes.

The force of his gaze struck her. Her breath punched out, and she could do nothing but stare back at him. The coolness was gone from his eyes, leaving a smolder she had never seen and couldn't make sense of.

Crow flopped on the floor between them, and Brodie's burning look vanished, leaving the Brodie who'd come to bring her brother's things back home—the man who'd seen atrocities unlike anything she could imagine.

"It's good to see you, Danica." His voice sounded as though sand was lodged in his throat. The gritty sound raised the hair on her forearms, and her nipples grew harder.

"Good to be back?" she ventured.

Resting his elbows on his knees once more, he dropped his head into his hands. When he scrubbed his jaw, a rasping noise sent her into a bigger spin than the F4 that had wiped out their town.

Finally, he raised his head. "I can't answer that yet. But it's good to be stateside."

There it was—that burning in his eyes again. It took the dark brown to a whole new level of intensity. She unfolded her legs and reached across the short distance to rest a hand on his arm again.

He let her touch him, offering a millisecond of comfort. The hair under her fingers was wiry and his skin warm. This was Brodie, not some stranger. They'd climbed trees together and fallen out of them too. He'd carried her, with a badly sprained ankle, to the house on his back. She'd cried so much she'd snotted on him, and he hadn't come near her for a week.

They were practically family.

Her throat clogged. "I hope you do stay, Brodie. I'm happy to see you."

Dropping his gaze to the bag between his boots, he made a noise in his throat that sounded like tearing paper. "I'm not sure you're going to be all that happy to see me."

She sat back, pulling her fingers into her lap and clenching them against the trace of heat lingering from his skin. A strange calm settled over her. She needed to see what was in the bag before her parents did, and Brodie seemed to know this. She and Matt had been so close. Inseparable. She'd cried for two weeks after he'd left. And when the phone call had come with the caller ID of "US Government", her heart had hit the floor.

But her parents…they were devastated to lose their only son. Matt would never again step foot on the land that was his birthright.

Brodie held her gaze deliberately, as if he could hold her up with the sheer force of his will. He picked up the bag and reached inside.

When the colors of the American flag came into sight, she burst. Tears exploded from her eyes and a sob rushed up her throat. Brodie hit his knees before her and wrapped her in his arms. She shook as she let him press her head down on his broad shoulder.

With a flick of his wrist, he unfolded the flag. It fluttered around them. Choking, she wrapped it around both of them, and they rocked in the combined pain of their monumental loss. She thanked God Brodie had been the one to bring Matt home.

Chapter Two

Brodie had been staring into the darkness for half an hour. It happened sometimes. He'd sit down to collect his thoughts and a long time later glance at his watch to see he'd lost another portion of his life.

He'd seen into the pits of hell and never cracked once. But holding Danica while she'd cried for her brother had nearly sent him off the deep end.

He was upset with Matt. Pissed, in fact. Matt had left him to do this dirty fucking thing—giving his family a bigger measure of pain than they'd felt upon hearing about the tragedy.

After several heartbreaking minutes, Danica had looked into Brodie's eyes and said, "Thank you for bringing him home."

Her parents had been harder yet to speak to, and well—he couldn't allow that memory to surface anytime soon. If ever.

Drawing a deep breath of the country air, he stopped hearing the constant loop of gunfire that played in his head day and night and focused on crickets and the faint buzz of mosquitoes. He swatted one.

Inside, a light burned in the kitchen, sending butter yellow squares across the porch boards. *God, what a fucking day.* The only good thing about it was the lingering scent of Danica's perfume on his clothes. Not just her perfume—*her.* That wild colt of a girl had grown into a beautiful and desirable woman.

Just thinking about her sent a pang of lust straight to his groin. More shit to tamp down and deal with. He couldn't touch Matt's baby sister.

30

Not a hint of a breeze blew. So much like the desert, but this place felt different and smelled different, and *he* was damn well different here.

Leaving behind the last five years and moving forward was his new mission. But what would he do to occupy his time? The ranch had enough work for him and Pa, he supposed, though it wouldn't be lucrative. How long before Brodie's money ran out?

A year maybe, if he lived frugally. A year in a dead town like this wouldn't be a picnic. There wasn't even a country bar where he could nurse a beer and shoot the shit with the guys.

The guys…what were they doing? Making plans as he was? At least they had each other.

The echoes of Danica's tears echoed his skull. Without thinking, he brought the neck of his T-shirt up to sniff. Pure, sweet woman.

Fuck, what was he thinking? She wasn't some uniform chaser looking to add another dog tag to her list of conquests. He might be a horny fuck, but he couldn't entertain thoughts of her big, ripe tits pressed so tight against her plaid shirt that the lines distorted. Or her smooth, tanned thighs he'd wanted to dive between and not surface for hours.

He bit off a groan and adjusted his cock.

The kitchen door cracked. "You all right, Brodie?" his momma asked quietly.

"Yes'm. Coming in now." He didn't move to get off the rocker, though. He stared into the darkness.

After the initial shock of having his son's dog tags in his hand, Mr. Pope had gotten to talking. At first it was mundane conversation as you would exchange at a funeral — about the weather, crops. The Popes were running about two hundred head of cattle. They had a lot of bulls, and that was one thing Brodie's family ranch was missing.

The screen door creaked shut. In the back of his mind, he noted his mother retreating into the house, leaving him.

That was good because he couldn't trust himself not to make a noise of despair as his mind moved on to Danica. How he'd reached into the bag a second time and placed the small, stuffed teddy bear into her hands. A bear she'd given Matt when he'd left for boot camp. Its furry paws were stitched to a red satin heart that said *I love you*.

Brodie bit down on his lip and shook himself. Then he got up and went inside. Going through the house, he shut off the lights his mother had left to guide him to his old bedroom. When he reached it, he kicked off his boots and started to yank his shirt over his head.

As he got a full whiff of Danica, he hesitated. Somehow, her nearness comforted. Maybe…just maybe it would keep the demons at bay long enough for him to catch a few winks. He threw himself into bed fully clothed and slept for eighteen hours.

* * * * *

Three solid days of rain. Danica had been wet to the skin again and again while doing ranch chores, which she didn't mind. It was the mud she hated.

The thick black earth stuck to everything. And dammit, these were her last pair of dry boots.

Using a stick, she worked to clean off the bottoms. When Crow barked, she looked up to see a figure crossing the field despite the soaking rain. Her heart skipped — Brodie. She'd know that rolling gait of his anywhere.

Watching him walk was like eating double chocolate fudge ice cream — decadent as hell. She savored every step he put down and the way his arms swung so naturally at his sides. His hat dipped so low over his eyes she couldn't see them until he mounted the porch steps.

"Brodie." Her voice was a little breathless, but she had a naturally raspy voice. Maybe he wouldn't notice.

"Are you catching cold in the wet?" Oh, he'd noticed, all right.

She shook her head, and droplets scattered over her shoulders. "I'm a country girl, remember? We don't catch colds from rain." She knew better than to be interested in a guy like Brodie. Unless he'd changed, he charmed everything with tits.

And she wasn't that kind of girl. Or was she? She *had* slept with Wayne on the first date. But that was different.

"Hmmph." Brodie took a seat next to her, and the old wooden chair creaked under his bulk. "Looks as if you've been making mud pies." He did a chin-nod toward the stick in her one hand and the boot in her other.

Her libido went into overdrive. Did the man do anything that wasn't sexy? She turned her gaze from his baby browns to his chest.

Damn, that was worse. He wore a faded denim shirt with pearl buttons. Rolled to the elbows, for the love of moonshine. She couldn't help but note the change a few days had made. He wasn't even wearing his dog tags.

"Nothing better to do than make mud pies on a rainy day."

He arched a brow, and her belly fluttered, low.

Dear Santa, I'll take a Marine…

"Your momma will skin your hide if you go in muddy," he drawled. For the first time since he'd come home, she saw him smile—a real smile that reached his eyes.

She swallowed hard. Giving up on the boots, she tossed the stick into the yard.

Brodie laughed. The sound rolled through her like thunder, shaking everything she knew about herself.

Apparently she wasn't really as content to be alone as she claimed.

"Crow didn't even go after that stick."

"Well, he's five years older and he's taken an aversion to the rain."

He laughed again, the sound so rich and full she could barely form a thought. "A cattle dog who hates the rain? Things really have changed around here."

His statement hung between them. "Yeah, they have," she said quietly.

He pushed to his feet and started pacing. She watched his long legs eat up the length of the porch several times before she caught his hand on the way past.

Scorching heat danced up her arm into her shoulder and threaded all the way through her. She forgot about her damp clothes and dripping hair. "Want to go inside for coffee?"

"Yeah, that'd be nice."

He was wet too, so in the kitchen, she handed him a towel. She squeezed the wet ends of her hair into the terrycloth, watching him pat rain off his shoulders and the brim of his hat.

Their gazes met.

There it was again—that low, dark heat.

She dropped her towel and he leaned against the counter.

"I didn't come here to stare at you, Danica. I'm sorry." What to say to that? She didn't have time to formulate a reply because he went on, "I came to make you a proposition."

So. Much. Worse. Visions of his hard mouth on hers as she tore off his wet denim shirt did a mad jig through her mind.

Before she said or did something stupid, she pushed him aside to get at the coffeemaker. "What sort of proposition?"

Was it her imagination or did his gaze lick over her backside? She didn't dare turn her head to see. Instead, she dumped two heaping scoops of coffee into the machine and added water. When she turned, he gave a small, nervous smile that quickly vanished.

"I have an idea."

"Just the one?"

"Hold your tongue, girl." His teasing lilt was returning—the one she'd missed so much when Matt and his friends had gone away. He leaned against the counter beside her. With only a foot separating them, she could feel heat radiating from the man.

"I've been thinkin' these past few days. Not much else to do with all the rain and my momma coddling me. Anyway, our ranch isn't doing too well, and from what I gather from your father, yours isn't either."

She gave a simple nod. "That's true." She'd seen the books herself. Lots of red ink there.

"The way I see it, we're neighbors and neighbors help each other out. Between us, we've got three hundred head of cattle. I've got a lot of cows that need calved. Our ranch was always a cow/calf enterprise, and we don't have a way to keep that going without bulls."

A thread of excitement wove through her. "And we've got bulls."

He nodded.

"I don't know why our fathers haven't done this before."

"Shell shock," he said as if it were obvious. "The storm, having cattle wiped out, the town gone. They've been just surviving." Their other loss hung between them, but he didn't voice it.

"I think you're right."

"I'm finished with just surviving, though. I'm ready to start living, and that means fixing our ranch first. And yours in the process. After we've got them up and running, I think we can hire some hands, bring blood back into Los Vista."

She blinked. It was a good idea. Better than good, actually. Exciting. "What do you want me to do?"

"Come with me to talk to your pa. If he's even up for talking."

"I don't know. He hasn't spoken a word since you were here the other day, Brodie."

His throat worked. "I'm sorry I had to do that, Danica."

"It was necessary. My parents have been different since... Well, c'mon. Let's go talk to Pa anyway."

An hour later, with a plan hammered out and another pot of coffee drunk between the three of them, she walked Brodie to the door. He fingered the brim of his hat in farewell. "Rain's supposed to clear tomorrow. I'll be up to work."

"We can start on that fence." The east side of her family's ranch had been touched by the high winds, and the fence was broken or falling over.

With a smile teasing the corner of his lips, he reached out and tweaked her ear. She yowled for show, but her body reacted to the touch as if it were a caress.

"Do you need anything before I go, Danica?" His warm eyes wore concern along with the usual strain she saw there.

"Got it covered, but thanks. Tomorrow bring your sledgehammer, Pup."

"Will do." His smile flashed far too briefly. He walked out the door, crossed the porch, and then walked across the field back to his ranch. She folded her arms over her chest, too aware of how he affected her. Wondering if Matt might forgive her if she accidentally slipped and landed right on Brodie Bell's cock.

She gave a small giggle. Before Brodie dropped out of sight, he turned and waved.

She waved back. And started praying for the rain to let up so she could spend the next day with him.

* * * * *

For five years, Brodie had barely been separated from his buddies. It seemed a few days was enough for them too, because he looked up to see the old blue Ford buzzing up the driveway, churning mud. Garrett stuck his head out the rear window and hooted.

Brodie couldn't help but laugh at the dumb shit.

By the time they hit the front porch, Momma was there with a smile and hugs for all. Then she bustled them inside for fresh cinnamon rolls and copious pots of coffee. Sitting in his kitchen with his friends was like old times.

Well, almost.

He scuffed his knuckles over his jaw and leaned back in his chair. "I've got something to tell you guys."

"We do too. We've got work clearing out some of the ruined buildings around town." Garrett poured himself another mug of rich, dark coffee. They didn't get coffee like this in a mess hall or a makeshift base camp.

"That was fast. A three-man crew?"

"We're hoping you can make it four."

"That's what I was gonna tell you. I've got some work ahead of me too. Right here on the ranch, and on the Popes' ranch."

The name of their platoon leader dropped into the room, silencing them. Then Wydell cleared his throat, and they all started talking at once.

"Is it true Matt's little sister's all grown up?"

"I heard she's a hottie. Might make me a trip over there today."

"I hear there's this schoolteacher in the next town over who's been trying to get a ring on her finger."

Brodie's head spun with all this information. A protective pressure built in his chest, and he leveled his gaze at Garrett, and then divided the rest of his stare evenly between Wydell and Boyd. "We ain't talking about Matt's sister that way. Show a little respect."

Garrett dipped his head first. "Yeah, you're right. So what's the plan with the ranch, Sergeant?"

"Combine them." His Texas twang was more pronounced now that he was home. It sounded good to his ears. "We lost our bulls in the storm and we need calves. The Popes have bulls and a lot of broken fence. We're going to combine efforts."

"Your father's on board with this?" Wydell rubbed his hands together, a nervous gesture he'd picked up in combat. The swishing noise reminded Brodie of holding his breath, of waiting for a kill shot. Adrenaline spiked in his system, and he started counting by fives.

"My pa's happy to let someone else take over for a while. And the Popes...well, you understand."

They nodded all around. For five minutes nobody spoke, drank, or nibbled one of his momma's cinnamon rolls. Time would have continued ticking by if Garrett didn't finally speak.

"After we get the debris cleared, we're going to put together a construction team."

"That's a hella-good idea. You think some of the residents will want to return?"

"We're hoping."

"But the businesses would take a lot to resurrect. There's nobody in town to even support the Chug-a-Lug." The bar where five of them had shared their first celebration of legal drinking age had been flattened.

Brodie shook his head, a weight settling over him again. "There's got to be a way to bring people back. New prospects."

"Yeah, but until that happens, the insurance companies are paying people to have their land cleared. We can do that."

"And I can get the two ranches left standing in the black again. Tomorrow Danica and I are mending fences."

Garrett's eyes twinkled.

Brodie reached out and cuffed his ear. "Stop thinking that way about Matt's sister. She's the same as always."

"Not what I hear," Wydell drawled.

That crawling sensation overtook Brodie again. "Just what have you been hearing?"

"That's she's as tall as a model with legs for miles."

That was true. "But who's saying it?"

"The whole county. I was thinking we should head up to the Popes' and pay our respects. I figure if we see her, it's a bonus."

Brodie pressed his lips into a line and tried to think of a way to deter his friends from visiting the Popes but couldn't think of any. They had as much right to be there as he did.

And if Danica took a liking to one of them...

"What about this teacher who wants to put a ring on her finger? Who is he?" He tried to sound cool, but his voice was strained. He wished like hell the guys didn't know him so well.

"The man talks about her all over town."

Damn.

"Saying what?"

Garrett raised a shoulder and let it fall. "We haven't met him, but anyone who knows us knows about Matt...and that means they know Danica. People say things because of the connection."

Brodie pushed away from the table. "If you're going to the Popes', I'll ride along."

"Nah, man, we can't go visiting right now. We're meeting someone about tearing into a barn." Garrett stood too and reached for a last cinnamon roll. As he bit into it, he eyed Brodie. "Soon, though."

Why the hell did Brodie feel so annoyed by that? He walked them to the car and rapped knuckles with each friend before tapping the roof twice in farewell.

He watched the old car move down the driveway, feeling immediately sad. This was a new chapter of his life, one without his brothers living on top of him. It felt strange. For five years, he'd breathed, sweat, and bled for his platoon. Now he was on his own with his demons.

Out in the barn, he spent some time feeding the few horses left on the ranch. If everything worked out in real life as it was in his mind, both ranches would be thriving by spring.

And then?

One step at a time. He'd been trained to always be prepared for the next step, but out here, he didn't need to be. He could take it easy. Sit in the porch swing for the rest of the night and listen to the peeper frogs singing their evening hymns.

He could walk up and see Danica.

All day he'd tried to convince himself he was so drawn to her because she was his last link with Matt, but that wasn't entirely it. She was more.

He shook himself and stroked the fuzzy white star between the horse's eyes. Brodie couldn't make out what compelled him to see Danica. Yeah, she was pretty. Gorgeous, actually. And with those legs for miles and waves of dark hair, she was beyond stunning.

He had a feeling she saw too deeply into him, and before long she'd be bugging him to talk about what he'd done in combat. So far his momma had cornered him twice.

Or maybe Danica would leave him be. She was easy to be around, maybe because they'd spent so much time playing as kids. Hell, he'd even skinny-dipped with her. He and Matt had been elementary age and Danica practically a baby. But he couldn't help but think of skinny-dipping with her now. He tried to shut the door on that thought before it ran out of control, but the wild horses broke free and galloped across the fields of his imagination.

Watching her drop her cutoff shorts over her hips, down her tanned thighs. Perky breasts disappearing beneath the cold spring water that fed the pond.

The hair on his arms stood up, but it had nothing to do with the memory of that cold swimming hole. He had too much time on his hands, and Danica was easy to fill it with. It was natural, when he hadn't had a girlfriend in too long to remember. She was handy, that was all.

Yeah, go on trying to convince yourself of that.

He gave the horse one final pat and left the barn. When he settled on the porch swing for a long, sleepless night, he stared in the direction of the Popes' place. And he longed for Danica's scent on his shirt.

Chapter Three

Watching Brodie set fence posts was going to be the death of her. He worked shirtless, the sun glistening off the sweat on his tanned skin. His back muscles rippled as he hefted the sledgehammer and swung.

Her sex drive felt as if it were on a racetrack, gearing higher and higher. Soon she'd skid out of control and grab his tight buns.

Or bite them.

"Hand me a couple of fork clips."

She jumped to action and fished in a tool pouch she wore around her hips for the clips. He tacked some barbed wire to the post with a V-shaped metal fastener. The strand wasn't broken, but they'd spliced together plenty so far. Replacing things cost money they didn't have, so they were making do.

"I think we have a love match."

He looked at her, a deep crease between his brows and confusion in his eyes.

She tipped her head in the direction of the cow and bull they'd put together that morning as a trial run. The bull was sniffing around the cow, and with her tail flicked to the side, she looked as wanton as Danica felt.

We poor ladies don't have a prayer.

Except Brodie definitely wasn't interested in her. All the perving was totally on her part.

Yes, she was a pervert. While Brodie set posts, she'd thought of ten ways for him to take her. Bent over the tailgate of the truck, hitched on the bumper. Facing him with her legs locked around his hips. Her hands tied behind her back as he pounded into her. And several scenarios of them in the tall grass. Hell, having hayseeds in her crack was well worth it for a few stolen moments with Brodie Bell.

She had his undivided attention at least. He wasn't sniffing around any females—there weren't any left.

He followed her gaze to the fence enclosure they'd trapped the cattle in. "They do look cozy."

"You know that old joke, don't you?" She waved a fly out of her face and moved down the fence line to the next tilted post. She pushed it upright in the hole and used her boot to kick some of the dirt around it.

He came at her with that swagger that probably was far from nonchalant. He knew damn well what he was doing. His walk, his dark good looks… She couldn't remember him having the same girlfriend for more than a week straight. What kind of sex life had he had in the service? She wasn't a dummy—men needed to slake their lust. She imagined hookers and probably a good share of girls between tours.

She had a handful of lovers notched on her leather belt too. Including that one-night stand with Wayne, the teacher in the next town. He kept texting and calling her, but she hadn't seen him a second time. It wasn't that the sex was terrible. She'd left his house very satisfied. And the conversation wasn't half-bad.

Yet she'd avoided more contact with him.

"What's the joke?" Brodie was asking.

She glanced back at the cattle. The cow trotted away with the bull in hot pursuit. Brodie swung around to watch too, his arm hooked around the post. They stood inches apart. If she leaned in, she could lick the bead of sweat on his tanned neck.

"A country boy and girl are standing in the field, watching the bull mount the cow. The boy says, 'Man, I wish I could be doing that right now.' And the girl says, 'You can go ahead and try. It's your cow. But I don't think the bull will like it.'"

Brodie tossed his head back and laughed. Laugh lines bracketed his hard lips and cut paths up to the corner of each eye. "What would your pa say if he heard you tell dirty jokes about cattle?"

"I'm not sure. I never told him one." She watched him laugh for thirty full seconds. Then it hit her—he didn't think of her as a woman at all. To him, she was a child. Matt's baby sister, tagging along wherever they went because she didn't have a playmate of her own.

Irritated, she twisted away. Out of the corner of her eye, she glimpsed the bull taking the cow.

Brodie took up the sledge and rapped the top of the post five times to set it in the earth. The barbed wire was still attached but sagging. He snipped it and wrapped the ends together with fence pliers to tighten it.

She stared down the row. "Only two miles to go."

"We've got the time."

"Nothing better to do." Her words sounded loaded even to her ears.

His glance was sharp, the furrow between his brows again. "How do you occupy your time?"

"Besides chores, you mean?"

He nodded.

"College courses online."

"Yeah? What're you going for?"

"Agricultural studies."

He made a noise of appreciation, which warmed her all over. Nothing sexier than a man who saw she had a mind, not just a nice ass in a pair of Levis. "So you want to ranch?"

She met his gaze. "It's my life. What else would I do?"

He raised a shoulder in a half shrug and continued to the next post. "Lots of things you could do, Danica."

Her name on his lips sounded far too sweet to her hungry ears.

"The military encourages us vets to go to school."

"Are you going to?"

"Dunno. Depends."

"On?" She swiped an errant lock of hair off her face, and he dragged his gaze over her.

"Whether or not we can get these ranches going again."

"If not?"

"I'll have to rethink everything. But I don't want to leave Los Vista."

She knew the feeling. After the storms, she'd stood along with the rest of the town, staring at the destruction and the loss of so many dreams. "I love this town. I don't want to be anywhere else." Her voice was strangely choked.

"You all right?" He scanned her face as if analyzing her emotional well-being. The moment wasn't unpleasant but it made her feel funny, as if he could look too deeply and see the woman inside who was broken after losing her brother and her town. Not to mention her parents who were so devastated by grief she could barely get them to eat or respond to her.

"I'm okay."

Brodie gave a nod. "Best get on then."

"Looks as if we might have a calf come spring." She waved toward the animals getting their happy on.

He stopped what he was doing to watch without a hint of embarrassment. "Ooh, Bessie, whattaya say we shake things up tonight?"

She laughed at the commentary. "Get on with it, Jack. I've got fifty more pounds of grass to eat today if you like my hips nice and wide."

Brodie pressed close to her, bringing the scents of a hardworking man. Not unpleasant by far. Her nipples hardened into tight buds. Unable to stop herself, she slid an arm behind his back, feeling the warm heat of his muscled spine. He slipped his arm around her too.

"Damn, Bess, you're tight."

A thrill ran through her at the odd dirty talk. "And you're packing some serious heat, Jack."

Laughing, Brodie looked down into her eyes just a few inches below his. *If only...*

He snaked his hand up her back and wrapped her ponytail around his fist. With a swift jerk, he pulled. She squealed. Se lunged for him and missed him by inches as he danced away.

Growling, she threw a playful punch, and it glanced off his arm. "Ow!" She cradled her hand against the pain rocketing upward.

"Shit. Didn't your brother teach you not to punch anything hard? You should always aim for soft spots."

"I don't see any soft spots on your whole body."

His jaw fell open, and he shut it with a snap. If her fingers didn't hurt so much, she'd probably laugh at leaving him speechless. She noted his chest puff out in pride, though.

He should preen a little—his body was perfection and he'd worked hard for it. She could only imagine the glory in his pants—

"Let me see." He cradled her fist on his palm and gently unfolded her fingers. In the pen, the cow gave a low *mooo* as the bull sealed the deal.

Brodie skimmed her fingers with the roughened pads of his own. "Can you move them?"

"Yes." She wanted to tell him she wasn't injured, but his touch felt too good. Now if only she could find a way to get him to touch her breasts…

Damn, she really was a perv. But he brought out an animalistic side of her and she had no idea how to stop it from surfacing. Or even if she wanted to.

He leaned so close the brim of his hat bumped hers. Still, he didn't move away, only stared down at her hand captured in his. "I'm sorry if I hurt you," he said.

"You didn't make me punch you."

"But I pulled your hair."

"Yes, you did." She gave him a very annoyed look, and he laughed.

"We should get to work."

"Will you come up to the house for lunch?" she asked.

He released her hand and put five paces between them. "Nah, Momma's got grub on for me. But thank you. Let's set these last five posts."

She rubbed her knuckles with her other hand, aware of the warmth lingering from his touch. Damn, she wanted him, Matt's best friend or not. Her body was a frantic cheerleader jumping up and down for him.

If he was going to think of her as a kid, maybe she should act like one. "Race ya to the next post."

For a moment she didn't believe he'd take the bait. He scuffed a boot over the ground. "Go!"

He got a head start, which made her howl at the injustice. And though his legs were a smidgeon longer, she was quick. She reached the goal at the same moment he did. He blinked at her for a second and then picked her up and set her down a foot behind the post.

"I won," he teased.

"You cheated."

"You didn't say anything about not cheating."

She pinched his nose—hard. He yelled and ducked away from her. She pursued him, and he tucked and rolled to escape her. She tumbled with him, fetching up by the post. When they both sat laughing, she couldn't stop staring at him.

Right now, she didn't detect the hard edge of pain he wore. He might be a carefree seventeen-year-old again. After a few seconds, the happiness in his eyes cooled, replaced by the devastation once more. She longed to reach out and comfort him. He'd come home to heal, but he was too busy making sure she was okay to worry about himself.

Beautiful, stubborn man. Guess I'll have to take care of him.

* * * * *

Watching Danica on horseback was a poetry he'd never be able to recite. She twisted in the saddle, searching for Crow. Her hat was low against the sun, her dark hair in long, free waves down her straight back. Her bare arms were tense as she reined in her horse.

God, she was strong and lovely. A real steel cowgirl.

And she had the same grit her brother did. While Matt had known how to lead men, Danica knew cattle. She spotted a wayward animal and sent Crow after it. The dog nipped at the cow's heels and it trotted back to the herd.

Brodie circled, never letting her leave his sight. Matt hadn't asked him to look after his little sister—he didn't need to. They were brothers in arms, their bond was forged in war. Danica hadn't battled with them, but she was Matt's blood, and she possessed the same steely disposition he had.

Part of him wished they were finished with the fence. Working so close to her was one hell of a strain, especially sporting a partial woody for hours on end.

He whistled, and Crow raced back to help. Brodie shook his head. Danica laughed as she danced her horse close enough to yell to Brodie. "When Crow runs cattle, he forgets he's old."

"I see that." It felt good to be in the saddle, surrounded by the animals and land. This was all he'd dreamed of in combat—the loamy field and a hard day's work. Of falling into bed at night with a sweet country girl in his arms.

Unfortunately he was living in a town that had about ten women residents, all too young, too old, or too ornery to start over. Except Danica.

She trotted ahead of him, giving him a tormenting view of her round ass bouncing in her saddle. Hell, he really needed to get a grip.

For over an hour they drove his cattle up to a spot on the Popes' land. Tomorrow they'd do the same with her cattle. Not to mention the miles of fence that still needed repair. There was no getting away from the sexy-as-sin woman. That meant he had to think of her differently.

He pictured the annoying girl who'd tagged behind him and Matt through the countryside. When they'd gotten on their horses to ride into town to spend a buck on a root beer, she'd trailed half a mile behind on her pony.

He pictured her ready for her first high school dance, hair in a long braid, her teeth encased in metal. She'd had her heart broken

68

by a boy, and Matt had rallied all the guys to put the fear of Jesus into the kid.

The cattle spotted the wide open space and ran for it. Danica slowed, and Brodie sidled up beside her. She shielded her eyes from the sun with one hand. The action brought her breasts forward, and he swam in very unbrotherly feelings for a full minute.

"There they go. Three hundred give or take a few couples in their motel rooms."

He laughed. She'd been calling the small corrals they'd set up the "Los Vista Motel". She'd always had a great imagination.

His imagination wasn't lacking either. He envisioned her roped to his four-poster bed. Over hay bales, in the back of his truck, and under the big Texas sky.

She tipped her head back to look at the sun. "Not quite lunchtime but I'm thirsty. Wanna go up to the house with me?"

The idea of going into the Popes' house and seeing her parents just sitting there in pain gave him a crawling feeling. His chest tightened, and he automatically started counting. "I've got a canteen here." He dug for it in his saddlebag. He opened the cap for her, and she reached for it. Their fingers brushed as she took the worn canteen.

When she brought it to her full, pink lips, he had to look away. His Wranglers tightened so much he feared his cock would strangle.

Once she lowered the canteen, she examined it. "Looks as if this has seen a rough life."

"Yeah, I carried it with me these past five years."

She turned it over to where a divot depressed the metal. "Did you use it as a shield?"

"Bullet ricochet." He heard the shots again. So many shots. *Ninety-two, ninety-three, ninety-four.*

She was staring at him, a soft look in her eyes.

All at once he snapped back to the present. His ears were filled with the lowing of cattle, and he was in the saddle again, far from combat.

"Do you want to talk about it?"

"Not particularly."

"I'm willing to listen. Except about Matt."

"No." His tone was so rough she winced. When she handed the canteen back to him and spurred her horse away, he felt the world close in on him. He watched her ride across the land they both loved.

Hell, he was fucked up. Was it getting worse by the day? He sure felt more haunted than he had a week ago. Adjusting to civilian life was no picnic for anybody, but being around Danica resurrected Matt's death even as it soothed Brodie.

He ran his hand over his face. Dammit, he needed to focus on work. Out here he forgot about his past for a little while.

He caught up to her. Their horses naturally swayed together, so close Brodie could touch her arm, warm from the sun.

"Let's stick to work, okay?"

"Sure."

"I know you don't want to hear the shit I could tell you."

"Maybe not, but it might ease you to say it." She didn't meet his gaze, just rode on, her body rolling with the horse's movements.

He pushed out a breath he'd been holding. "Why don't I go home for a while and we'll meet at the barn after lunch?"

As she swung her gaze in his direction, his mind was caught in a whirlpool and dragged down into all the sweet goodness of Danica Pope. He wrapped his fingers around her wrist, and their gazes locked.

72

With supreme effort, he released her wrist and spurred his horse. Over his shoulder, he called, "See you."

"Later, Pup."

* * * * *

"Pa, I need some cash for feed." Danica stared at her father as he went through the motions of working in the barn, but he wasn't really present. When he didn't answer, she said, "Pa?"

He waved at her. "Use the card, honey."

"We can't keep putting money on the credit card. Isn't there any cash in the checking account?"

"You pore over those books every day. You tell me."

Yeah, they were broke. They'd usually have some cash flow from selling some three-hundred-pound young'uns. But they hadn't taken any to auction—they'd missed the big yearly one in Abilene because of Matt. Her pa didn't have the heart for ranching right now. Or anything, really.

"Okay, I'll use the card." It was never so apparent to her that she and Brodie couldn't fail. They needed to make a go of this crazy scheme of his.

On her way out of the house, she caught her mother standing at the sink just staring out the window. Danica put a hand on her shoulder. Her momma didn't move. Leaning in, she pressed a kiss to her thin cheek.

Danica's heart ached not only for her brother but for her parents. She understood what they were going through, but it was breaking her down on a daily basis.

When she started toward her truck, she saw the cloud of dust moving up her driveway. A small thrill hit her belly.

In seconds Brodie had parked the Bells' truck and jumped out. His boots were dusty, his jeans slung low on his hips. His old belt buckle was worth studying just to keep staring at the delectable transition between hard abs and hips.

He wasn't wearing a shirt, damn him.

The shit-eating smile toyed with the corner of his mouth and finally won. He grinned.

"What're you smiling about, Pup?" Her insides quivered.

He spoke, but damn if she could focus on any words coming out of that sexy mouth. He was so distracting, in fact, that she didn't see the other truck pull in or the man get out.

Brodie's face changed, and he glared over her head. "You got company."

She pivoted to see Wayne striding toward her, a bouquet in his grip. Wildflowers, the stems all different lengths. So charming, yet…

She flushed as Wayne leaned in to give her the bouquet and kiss her cheek in greeting. "I had an appointment and left class early. I thought I'd drive up here and see how you've been."

In other words, she wasn't answering his calls or texts, so he was going to force her to respond face-to-face.

"Uh, hi Wayne. Thank you. These are beautiful." They were and any country girl would be honored to have a man picking flowers for her and making a long drive to deliver them. So what was her problem?

Brodie cleared his throat. He reached around her to shove his hand at Wayne to shake. "Brodie Bell."

"Ah, I've heard about you and your buddies making it home."

Brodie's expression became guarded. Wayne's smile wavered at Brodie's stern look. Danica studied Brodie. Her guess was he didn't want to talk about his time as a soldier, and definitely not with a stranger.

"Yeah, thanks." He gripped Wayne's hand and pumped it hard. "I'll leave you two to talk." He started to walk away, and Danica panicked at the thought of him leaving.

Or of being trapped with Wayne.

"Wait, Brodie. I thought we were heading over to town for some feed."

He stopped in his tracks and looked at her. She hoped her plea wasn't written all over her face. She hated to hurt Wayne's feelings, but...

Brodie gave a nod and walked back. He reached into his open truck window and pulled out his T-shirt, which he drew on with such mesmerizing slowness she almost issued a mewl of lust.

"Well, thanks again for the flowers, Wayne. Brodie and I need to get on the road." She walked around Brodie's truck and got into the passenger's seat. Brodie looked in the window at her. A question was in his eyes, and she knew she was in for it. He'd demand to know who Wayne was to her and why she was so eager to escape.

Brodie hopped in and started the engine. He backed out and raised a hand in goodbye to the poor schoolteacher.

Leaning against the seat, Danica released a heavy sigh.

"Wanna talk about that?"

"No." It was her turn to sound short and gruff.

"A boyfriend of yours?"

"A teacher I saw once."

"You slept with him." Brodie's words made her jerk. Without a glance at her, he pulled onto the desolated road that led to their dead little town.

"I—" She started to protest and thought better of it. He'd see through her anyway. "Okay, I did."

"And now he wants more but you don't?"

"I don't want to talk about it, Brodie."

"Huh. I know that song and dance, princess."

His pet name for her sank deep into her body, past any reservation about him being Matt's friend. Her lips fell open.

He did a double take at her. "Dammit." He whipped his truck off the road into a parking lot with the ruins of a dentist's office. He put the truck in park and they stared at each other across the cab that suddenly felt tight and cramped.

"I'll tell you all about it as soon as you let out some of your demons," she challenged.

He narrowed his eyes. "Who says I have demons?"

"I see you counting to yourself. Do you think I don't know you're trying to talk your anxiety away?"

"You read lips now?"

"Maybe I do. You can't hold that darkness inside you forever, Brodie. It will eat you alive and you'll be worthless to your friends, your parents, the ranch and even—"

"Danica," he said, cutting her off.

"Yeah?"

"Shut up."

She opened her mouth to protest but he grabbed her nape and yanked her across the console to meet him. When his lips crashed over hers, she gasped. The wildflowers she'd been clutching dropped from her fingers and she closed her hands over Brodie's shirt. Bringing him as close as she could get him.

Fucking hell, he had a serious case of blue balls. So much for distancing himself from her. As soon as he'd seen the way Wayne had looked at her, Brodie's inner alpha was prepared to mark his territory. He'd wanted to throw Danica behind him to keep the guy's eyes off her.

Angling his head, he drew her deeper into his kiss. He ran his tongue over her sweet, plump lips, and she opened to him with a moan he felt deep in his body.

Her hat had fallen off with the first brush of his lips, and he filled his fingers with all that fucking glorious hair. Porn star hair. He wanted to wrap it around his fists and plow into her tight, sexy body.

When she touched her tongue to his, a growl shook loose from his core. He latched an arm around her and half-lifted her from her seat before realizing what he was doing.

Ravishing Matt's baby sister.

He tore his mouth free. She dropped back into her seat, eyes blurry and her lips swollen from his kisses.

"Hell," he grated out.

"Brodie…"

"Don't say it. Please. I already know. I'm sorry. I don't have any right to put my hands on you. You're practically my little sister."

She groaned and dropped her face into her hands. "Don't say that."

Anger boiled up and filled his chest. With a jerk, he put the truck in gear and whipped into the road, right in front of Wayne.

"Jesus, don't kill him."

He shot Danica a look. He stomped on the gas and put a good half a mile between his truck and Wayne's.

"So you slept with him. How many times?"

"What business is it of yours?"

He'd forgotten about her sass until now. "My job is to make sure my friend's sister is behaving."

She snorted. "What can you do about it?"

"I'll lock your ass up in the woodshed if I have to."

She folded her arms over her breasts and shot him a look packing more heat than a fifty-caliber machine gun. "I'm an adult, not some kid you need to watch over."

As he glared at her, taking in curves that would give a man whiplash, deep eyes, and sultry lips, he lost his train of thought. Yeah, she was pure woman.

He shook himself. "How much feed do we need anyhow?"

"What? You're changing the subject?"

"Hell yeah."

"I'm not telling you until we get there."

"Fine."

She turned her head to look out the window and he locked his attention on the road, the ruins of Los Vista, and the sky. Anywhere but Danica. And he sure as hell wasn't going to relive that kiss.

Two miles down the road he'd replayed it in his mind nine times. Damn, what had he gotten himself into? He was in quicksand with no way of climbing out.

Chapter Four

There was only one thing worse than a grumpy cowboy, and that was a cowboy who was wet to the skin—at least to her libido. Danica had been working with Brodie for an hour, and every damn move he made was making it hard to look away. Or work for that matter. "Can't we just knock off for a few hours until the rain lets up?"

Brodie raised his head, water running off his hat, and stared at the fence. They'd managed to erect a lot of posts even in the rain, so she understood his hesitation. It was just that if his jeans got any wetter, she couldn't be held accountable for her actions.

A shiver ran through her.

"Are you getting cold?" Concern punctuated his brows.

"No." *I'm too damn hot*. But she couldn't exactly say she wanted to jump his hard body and lick the rain off his skin. Could she?

"If you need go back up to the house, I won't think less of you." His teasing tone was reflected in the smile tipping the corner of his lips.

To prove how much she didn't need to go to the house, she gripped a post and began to wrangle it into an upright position. He watched her struggle for a second before moving toward her.

His body rolled, his wet shirt clinging to his broad shoulders. When he grasped the post and added his strength and body weight, the post jerked in the opposite direction. She wasn't one of those women who believed she could do everything herself, but it irritated her that he'd managed it so easily.

He gave her a long look. Goose bumps broke out on her forearms. Damn, why did he look like the most delicious dessert ever while she had to look like a drowned rat? Her top was molded to her like a second skin and her hair hung in a wet, dripping tail down her back.

"I'll fill in the dirt around this hole. You get the next post," she said.

Her words made his eyes clear. As he turned to do her bidding, she wondered where his mind had been just then. At times she drifted off into memories of them as kids, playing with Matt. She knew Brodie did too.

Just yesterday he'd spent twenty minutes recounting tales of how annoying she'd been. The time she'd shown up at the pond where they'd taken some dates and asked why they didn't want to hang out with her. When she'd tried to jump out of the hayloft and had sprained her ankle—again.

The thing still ached, especially in weather like this. As a kid, she'd practically lived in an ankle wrap.

As she began to shovel earth into the hole around the post, she watched Brodie from the corner of her eye. He'd moved down the fence line. The posts were leaning at all angles, many stuck, baked into the Texas ground.

With a grunt, he shoved one. It gave way immediately. The look he tossed her raised a deep ache low in her belly, along with thoughts of his thorough, mind-bending kiss.

"Dammit," he muttered and moved to the next post. The rain started to fall faster. She watched the water soak his spine, right between those beautiful bulges of muscle.

While she filled in the dirt, she couldn't tear her gaze away from him. The fierce expression he wore coupled with the way he manhandled the wood left her with a feeling that he was waging a mental war.

He must have seen and done some horrific things in the name of his country. Not all soldiers had outlets for their frustrations like Brodie did. At least he could throw himself into hard work.

Then he hit a post he couldn't move.

He threw himself at it. Veins stood out on his neck, and he bared his teeth as he tried to force it upright.

She stood back and watched him go at it again and again. Nothing happened.

Crowding beside him meant her boots sank into a sticky mud hole. But she didn't care.

"What are you doing?" he asked, panting hard.

She placed her hands beside his on the wood. "Helping."

He gave her a sharp nod. "On three. One, two, three." They went at it together. For five solid minutes they tried to move that post.

"It hasn't budged an inch," she rasped, falling back.

"Not a millimeter." He rapped his gloved knuckles off it.

She was breathing hard.

Brodie scowled at her heaving chest. "Go on back to the house. I'll finish up here."

Turning, she noted another two hundred yards of fence to fix. Not a lot when your hands weren't slipping on wet wood or you weren't shoveling mud. But in this filthy weather, the idea of a warm house and dry clothes worked its magic on her senses.

"Let's go in and have some coffee. Dry off."

His eyes bulged a little. Shaking his head hard, he said, "Nope. I'm finishin' this. You go on up."

She settled a hand on her hip. "Brodie. If you're hell-bent on working, there's stuff to do in the dry barn."

"Jesus, does she know what she sounds like?" His murmur reached her through the constant patter of rain. He started attacking the post again with more vigor than before.

She watched him for a minute. Finding no words to convince him, she turned and walked away. Across the field and back toward the ridge where the house seemed to snooze under the gray sky.

Once she saw the windows with all the curtains drawn, she stopped in her tracks.

Damn, she'd forgotten her home was now like a funeral parlor. Her parents were devastated and grieving. They spoke in hushed whispers and barely stepped into the sun. Matt wouldn't have wanted this for them, but what was Danica to do? They needed time. If her pain was so raw and fresh, she couldn't imagine what her parents must be feeling.

But she didn't want to go inside just yet.

Heading to the barn was the natural decision. Inside was dry and smelled of fresh hay. A few horses greeted her with whickers, and a cat came to curl around her ankles—until it discovered how wet she was.

It skittered away, and she laughed.

Now that she was out of the rain, she realized how soaked her clothes really were. She should at least go into the house and get a fresh set, but the idea of being dry while Brodie was out there drenched didn't set well.

Some of those posts seemed cemented into place. Nothing would move them except...

She spun to the barn door and opened it to stare at her truck parked a good, fast sprint away. The only thing that might move those posts.

And get Brodie's stubborn ass out of the rain.

She slapped the front of her jeans, feeling for her truck keys. Then she took off running across the wet yard. Minutes later she was driving toward the fence line where Brodie was still taking out his anger on the same post.

When she laid the heel of her hand on the horn, he looked up, his face blanking. Then a huge grin spread, and she felt it echo in the walls of her heart.

By the time she pulled up beside him and rolled down her window, her pulse had galloped out of control. Seeing him smile, knowing she'd put it there...well, it made up for so much pain in her life right now.

She grinned at him. "Need some horsepower, cowboy?"

"Could use a little, yeah. You got rope?"

"In the back." She twitched her head in the direction. As he walked to the back of her truck, she watched him in the side mirror. Even with the reflection mottled by streaming rain, he was damn fine. Her nipples were as hard as pebbles, and only half the reason was her wet, cold shirt.

He appeared at her window again, hat dark with rain and his eyes even darker beneath it. With his five o'clock shadow and dirt smeared on his cheekbone, he looked rugged as hell.

She released a slow, even breath.

"I hooked the rope to your hitch. Pull forward until I say stop."

Unable to fabricate a real word, she simply nodded. He stood back to watch the progression. She settled her boot on the gas and gently depressed the pedal. The truck rolled, and she felt the rope catch.

"Keep goin'," Brodie called.

She did.

"It's moving! Coupla more feet." His face, which had just been creased in frustration, was now wreathed in smiles. Something inside her broke open, as warm and sweet as honey. She liked seeing him happy. Making him happy.

"Whoa!"

She braked, and Brodie waved at her while he went to check the post. A second later he was at her window again.

"Think you can go forward about six inches?"

"Are you suggesting I can't drive?"

He scrubbed his gloved finger beneath his nose. "Not at all. Just go forward until I tell you to stop."

She couldn't help but admire his backside as he resumed his place.

"Go on." He waved.

She repeated the process. When he called for her to stop, she was distracted by his damn pretty face and bent the post the wrong direction.

"Whoa! You're too far."

Biting her lip, she put the truck in park and got out. "This wouldn't have happened if you would have come up to the house for that coffee."

He blinked at her as if she were speaking in tongues. "You're the one who came back."

She stared at his mouth for two heavy heartbeats. Was it too much to stop for coffee? And why hadn't he tried to kiss her again? Days had passed and he hadn't even looked at her as a man looks at a woman.

When she reached the post, she shook her head. "It's barely left of center."

"Still crooked."

"Who knew you were a perfectionist, Brodie Bell?" Rain showered both of their heads. She wanted a warm, dry bed and this man in it with her.

"You knew. Remember when I practiced ropin' that summer?"

She groaned. "God, yes. You made me stand in the yard while you lassoed me from all angles. Half the time you hit me with the rope. I swear I still have red marks."

He let his gaze dip over her wet form. His lips compressed and he glanced away. "Sorry about that, but you wanted to help."

"No, I wanted to be with you and Matt no matter what you were doing. I let you rope me so I could stay close to you." Her words splashed between them.

He dragged in a deep breath before spinning away. "I'll finish these up. Thanks for bringing the truck."

As he stomped to the next post, she issued a groan of frustration. The man needed to work out some demons? Let him. But it seemed like plain old stubbornness to her.

Working closely with a woman in a wet shirt molded to her breasts was bad. But she was wet all over, and that made Brodie want to peel her clothes off and tuck her into a warm, dry bed.

With him.

Son of a bitch. Matt's voice popped into his mind, and Brodie almost bit his tongue, which was practically hanging out as he watched Danica's ass twitch away from him. She got into the truck and slammed the door.

When she laid on the gas and threw mud clumps off the tires at him, he knew he was in trouble. Wet, angry women were forces to be reckoned with.

He had no choice, though. He had to keep shoving her away or she'd burrow too close and he'd end up kissing her again. Or worse.

For days since their shared kiss, he'd been eating, sleeping, and breathing Danica. Hell, she'd haunted his dreams and he'd awakened with a boner the size of a bazooka. He'd had no choice but to take care of his needs—twice—before it would fit in his jeans. But this couldn't go on.

As a senior his buddies had teased him that she liked him. Of course, being a jackass at that age, he'd said within her hearing that he'd rather kiss his horse than Matt's kid sister. And watched her face crumple before she turned away.

She hadn't talked to him for weeks after that. In fact, she'd gone steady with a big jerk who had told the whole school he'd slept with her. That had roused Matt's anger, and, in turn, Brodie's. The five of them had marched up to the boy and made him taste the inside of his locker.

After that, Brodie's friendship with Danica had been a little easier.

Still, what he'd said wasn't true today. No way would he rather kiss his horse. Her sweet lips were turning him inside out.

As he righted five more fence posts, his mind wandered to Matt. His platoon leader and best friend wouldn't want Brodie schmoozing on his baby sister. Besides, Danica was all light and hope while Brodie was filled with darkness. The times he woke and bolted

up in bed, a scream of horror on his lips…
Well, he couldn't drag her into that hell with
him.

By the time he finished the portion of fence
and walked back to the house, he was in a
mood. Covered in mud and soaked to the skin,
unable to have what he wanted. He was man
enough to admit he was acting like a grumpy
little kid.

Danica was in the barn, dry, her fluffy hair
a dark cloud around her shoulders. He raked
his gaze over her curves. Even in old jeans and
a hoodie, she was beyond sexy.

I have to get some distance.

"I'm going on home for the day."

She turned at his voice, hand still
outstretched to the horse she was treating to a
couple apple slices. Her lips turned down at
the corners. "You should get out of those wet
clothes."

He ground his teeth against the images her words evoked. "That's why I'm headed home."

"But you aren't coming back? There's still plenty of daylight. We can talk about where we're getting the money to patch the fence between our properties." She was hatless, and it took everything in him not to close the gap between them and sink his hands into her thick hair. Tip her face back and kiss her sultry lips.

For long seconds he worked through his mental imaginings before focusing on what she was saying. They'd planned to open the fence on his family's ranch and patch the Popes' fence into it, creating one big enclosure.

Not that anybody was left to care if the Bell and Pope herds wandered onto their lands. But since a young age Brodie had been taught the family creed—trust everyone but brand your cattle.

Across the space, he stared at Danica. The longer he looked, the tighter his chest became.

And his jeans.

"I gotta go," he said gruffly.

"Wait, Brodie."

He hadn't even moved a muscle yet she was calling him back. This wasn't going to end up good, if the look on her face was anything to go by. She wore the same wide-eyed expression she had after he'd kissed her in the truck.

When she walked toward him, his muscles stirred, as if knowing he should run. But he stood rooted to the old wood floors.

She placed a hand on his arm, and he swallowed hard. "Look, I know you struggle. I can see it in your face."

"What?" Did she know he was thinking about lifting her and impaling her on his cock?

"The war does things to people. It must weigh on you a lot."

He almost breathed a sigh of relief. She thought he was battling the aftermath of war when really he was fighting desire for her.

Traumatic stresses were a very real thing—but right now, Danica was a bigger force.

He wanted her.

He couldn't touch her.

But she's touching me.

He shook his head and pulled his arm free of her grasp. "I told you I can't discuss that stuff with you."

"I know, but Matt would have wanted me to listen."

Anger built inside him for no good reason besides the fact that his best friend was dead and standing between him and the woman Brodie lusted after. "Leave him out of this."

"You can't even say his name, can you?" Her eyes swam with tears, but Brodie had a feeling they were more for him than her brother.

"Just...don't. I don't need a counselor." His harsh tone stopped her like a bulletproof vest.

She dropped her arms to her sides and her shoulders slumped. "Fine."

"Aw, Danica, I'm sorry."

"Go out with me. We need to get out of here. Let's do something."

He eyed her. Dammit, after working long days he shouldn't want to spend more time with her, yet that's all he could think of.

"Maybe another time," he said.

Her disappointment was quickly masked. "Fine, you stubborn ass. Head on home then."

Now that she'd told him to, he couldn't. He stood stock-still. They stared at each other. When she tore her gaze away, his heart rolled over painfully.

It's best.

"I'll see you tomorrow, Squirt."

She lifted a brow but didn't otherwise respond to his nickname.

Feeling so off his game wasn't normal. For five years he'd given his all. He'd tackled life with every ounce of determination he possessed. Now he couldn't allow himself to.

When he left the barn, a fragile cord somewhere deep inside snapped. His throat burned and his legs ached to go back, to grab her and make her understand.

Understand what, though? He didn't quite know himself.

The sky hung low and dark. More rain threatened. During storms as kids they'd go in the house and watch cartoons, sprawled on the furniture and rugs. Danica always claimed the beanbag chair and a patchwork afghan. What Brodie wouldn't do to have those times back, a time when she was just Matt's kid sister.

Not the woman of his friggin' dreams.

* * * * *

As Danica pulled the baking sheet of snickerdoodles from the oven, she leaned over to inhale the scents of cinnamon and sugar. Memories flooded her mind, and she suddenly stopped with the tray in midair.

Her eyes swam as she stared at Matt's favorite cookies. When she'd mixed the batter, she'd only been thinking of comfort food and maybe sharing a few with Brodie. Now that she was faced with the thick memories, she couldn't deal.

If she couldn't deal, her parents really couldn't. She darted a glance around, but they were nowhere to be seen. Thank goodness.

Crossing the kitchen, she hit the back door with her shoulder and shoved outside. The pig shed wasn't far, but she was desperate to get rid of these cookies.

Since the day Brodie had brought the flag and teddy bear, she hadn't really broken. She was too distracted by hard work and manly muscles. Now she was faced with the greatest loss of her life all over again.

She tipped the cookie sheet, flinging the still warm snickerdoodles to the far reaches of the pigpen. It didn't take long for the fat animals to sniff the treat and come waddling after them.

Which only made her giggle. She rubbed her tears away with the oven mitt she was still wearing. God, what a mess she was.

Turning for the house again, she looked out over the land. What she saw were even fence posts running as far as the eye could see. Pride filled her. They'd done this—she and Brodie. While the town struggled and her parents were trapped in pain, she and Brodie had actually achieved something.

In the kitchen, her mother was staring at the bowl of batter Danica hadn't yet baked.

Crap.

"I'll just give this to the pigs, Momma."

Her mother blinked but didn't respond.

Five happy pigs later, Danica was washing out the bowl in the empty kitchen. She didn't know where her mother had gone, and she wasn't going looking. If she witnessed more tears, how could she remain strong?

She needed something to do, and Brodie had made it clear he didn't want to do anything with her. Her few friends from Los Vista were living in the neighboring town. She could call them and meet at the local honky-tonk.

When she picked up her cell, she saw two missed calls from Wayne. The guy was persistent, she'd give him that. And if Brodie wasn't interested, what was she waiting around for?

As she listened to his voicemails, her mind looped from Brodie's scorching kiss to the pigs devouring the sweet morsels to her one-night stand with Wayne.

Yes, she definitely needed to get out of there. She was going stir-crazy, and she knew herself well enough to know that it wasn't a good idea to sit around. When the deep restlessness took hold, she needed to move.

She stabbed a fingernail into her cell and shot off a text to her girlfriend. *Want 2 go out?*

Can't. I'm out of town with Michael.

Disappointment spread through her, but she responded to her friend with a good luck clover. Her other friend was also a dead-end. As Danica flipped through her contacts list, Wayne messaged.

How's my favorite cowgirl?

She bit her lip. Maybe he wasn't so bad. Actually, he was nice. She didn't know what was holding her back. He was good-looking and stable.

Fine how are u?

His response flashed in seconds. *Hoping to see you. Want to go riding?*

Horseback riding was tempting as hell. She loved to ride for pleasure, and Wayne had told her about the trails around his house.

Meet me. You won't regret it.

She wasn't going to sit here bored and dwelling on the past—or a future with a stubborn ex-soldier turned cowboy who'd kissed her once.

Okay. I'll meet you at Shooters in an hour.

Several smiley faces appeared on her screen. "Guess that's a yes," she said to herself.

She went to her bedroom and starting rummaging through her closet. She needed an outfit appropriate enough for drinks and comfy enough for riding. She tossed out several items and took less than a minute to decide on her slimmest dark jeans and a black top that hung off one shoulder.

Wearing it meant she had to change out of her everyday white bra and into something with a slinky strap. "But I need to hold the girls up," she muttered, rooting through a drawer.

She held up a bra and examined it. Dammit, cowgirls really had it bad when it came to undergarments. She wanted to be cute but not bounce. Her options were limited. With a sigh, she wiggled out of her clothes and into the bra and matching panties. When she looked down at her bare toes, she groaned.

The polish was chipped. Sure, she'd be wearing boots but what if…?

She threw on the rest of her clothes, grabbed her bottle of Bombshell Beauty nail polish and went back out into the kitchen where the lighting was better. She had just propped her foot on the stool and had the tiny brush aimed at her big toe when the kitchen door opened.

Glancing up, she nearly swallowed her tongue.

Brodie Bell in a Marine Corps T-shirt and clean jeans. He was wearing a black cowboy hat instead of his regular battered brown. *Of course he is. His other hat's soaked.*

His gaze raked over her from head to chipped toenail.

"What are you doing here?" she asked. To keep from gawking at him, she applied the first brushstroke of vampy red over the old layer.

"I just dropped off some feed. We had a few bags sitting around in our barn and I remembered your chickens were out."

"Oh. Thanks." She polished her second toe then third. When he didn't leave, she stole a glance at him. "Why are you so dressed up?"

"Why're you?"

She finished her right foot and propped up her left. "No reason. Just thought it would be nice to get out of my grubby barn clothes for a change."

"The guys and I are going to rip up the next town. Since this one's already flattened."

Her stomach lurched at the realization that he wasn't against going out—just going out with her.

"Well have fun," she said coolly.

His crooked smile was far too bad-boy for her rioting hormones. "We'll see what fun we can find, but don't worry. We won't be stupid." She snorted and settled her foot on the floor. He dropped his gaze to her toenails. "Nice color."

"Thanks."

"I might get a late start tomorrow morning."

"Me too," she blurted. Maybe she should just tell him she was going out with Wayne. Nah—he'd had his chance. She lifted her jaw. "I might sleep in, but I'll let Pa know so he can feed and water the cattle."

"Sounds good." Brodie sniffed the air. "Do I smell snickerdoodles?"

Compressing her lips, she nodded. "I wasn't thinking."

"About?" He really was clueless. Maybe it was a man thing or she was just overly sensitive. Probably both.

"Matt's favorite."

Brodie's face transformed. Tension bracketed his lips and his eyes darkened, if such a thing were possible. His eyes were already espresso. "I remember now. You okay, Squirt?"

She didn't want to face this interrogation. She wanted to stuff her head in the sand and not think about all the uproar in her life right now. "As long as you're not calling me Easter, I'm good."

His face cracked into a grin, but it didn't quite reach his eyes. "All right then. Catcha later, Danica."

As Brodie left her kitchen, she no longer detected the cinnamon scent of cookies. No, she smelled clean aftershave and leather. She sighed. This was going to be a long night if she didn't screw her head on straight. Wayne deserved a chance, didn't he? And she needed some fun.

Trouble was, her idea of fun had just walked out the door.

* * * * *

"Welcome home, boys." The old guy holding down the barstool turned to salute Brodie and his friends as they sauntered up to the bar.

"Thank you, sir." Brodie probably shouldn't have worn his Marine Corps T-shirt. It invited conversation he didn't want right now. Thinking of Danica at home baking Matt's favorite cookies and trying to keep the hurt look off her face twisted Brodie up inside.

"Let me buy you boys a drink in appreciation for your service." The old guy waved at the bartender, a slim little blonde wearing shorts and a midriff top. His ears buzzed with talk and music. He barely registered his friends telling the bartender their orders or her wide smile for him.

"Same," he muttered. When he had his beer in hand, he made his way through line dancers to a table toward the back. He wanted to hide in the shadows and watch people have fun while he thought of how to get the same for himself.

"What crawled up your ass, Pup?" Garrett swung his chair backward and straddled it. He brought his bottle to his lips.

"Nothin's wrong." He drank off half his bottle at once.

His friends settled around him, staring at him as if he'd grown a spare head.

"What?" He didn't mean for his tone to come out in that barking military command, but it was second nature.

"That bartender was crushing on you hard, Pup. Why aren't you hittin' that?" Garrett pivoted to look back at her. Brodie followed his gaze and sure enough, the blonde was smiling at him.

He turned away. "I'm not up for that."

"Why the hell not? Your pecker get shot off and I didn't hear about it?"

The guys sniggered. The familiar sound gave Brodie a measure of peace, and he found himself smiling too. He leaned his elbows on the table and turned his bottle around and around in his hands.

As they talked about what they'd been doing to help Los Vista—clearing broken trees and cleaning up collapsed buildings—Brodie's mind kept wandering back to the Pope Ranch. He could talk about all the fence they'd fixed and how they were ready for stage two of their plan. But everything he thought to say had Danica's name attached.

And he thought of her far too much already.

Wydell waved at a passing waitress. "Time for something a little harder. Whiskey all around."

Brodie opened his mouth to decline, but he caught sight of the couple moving toward the dance floor.

He jerked to his feet so fast the table wobbled. Everyone stared at him, including the waitress. Ignoring them, he gawked at the familiar face. No, the stunning, breath-stealing beauty — the one with a man's hand planted on her lower back as he steered her through the crowd.

"Two whiskies," he grated out. He dropped back into his seat and continued to stare at Danica and the teacher. Her body was angled away from Brodie so he couldn't see her face, but it was definitely Danica. He'd know that body anywhere.

And he knew she was wearing a sexy dark red toenail polish. She'd painted her damn toenails for a date.

"Fuck."

His three friends riveted their attention to him as the waitress moved away.

"What the fuck are you seeing that we aren't, man?" Garrett's question was one he'd heard before while peering down his scope at an enemy.

He gave a swift shake of his head and gritted his teeth against the need to shout for that guy to take his hands off Danica.

Matt's little sister.

The woman who had Brodie's cock as hard as steel twelve hours a day.

Son of a bitch. She lied about going out tonight.

Now she was going to line-dance with him.

No. Fucking slow dance with him.

The tune changed to an old Dolly Parton ballad, and Danica was wrapped up in another man's goddamn arms.

At that moment the waitress set two whiskies before him. "Good timing," he drawled, gripping a glass.

The first drink was a salute to his friends, all they'd lived through together, and to rebuilding new lives. The second drink was essential to suppress the vision of Danica with the teacher.

While they whirled to Dolly's feminine crooning, Brodie watched, trying to glimpse Danica's face. If he could see her smile and know she was happy, that would be enough for him.

"What the hell, Brodie?" Wydell asked, craning to see what Brodie was staring at.

"Nothin'. Let's drink."

"We already did. Welcome back to planet Earth," Wydell quipped.

"Looks like I still have a drink. I'd better remedy that." He cupped the glass and raised it to his lips. At that moment the teacher spun Danica. Across the bar her gaze locked on Brodie. Panic crossed her lovely features.

He tossed back the whiskey and while it burned a path straight to his stomach, he stood. Crossing the room to her was easy — people parted to let a big man through. What would take some work was controlling himself. The alcohol hit his bloodstream just as he tapped Wayne on the shoulder.

"Can I cut in?"

* * * * *

Oh God, Brodie. No.

Danica could see the fight in the tension in his shoulders and the set of his square jaw. The jagged scar she barely noticed anymore stood out white against his tanned face.

"It's up to the lady." Though Wayne's words were smooth, his tone wasn't.

She ripped her attention from the pissed-off Marine to Wayne's face. She patted his shoulder to soften her decision. "I won't be long."

He released her. His hands had barely left her waist and hip when Brodie dragged her right up against his hard body. She sucked in a gasp.

"You reek of whiskey already. I thought you were going to be sensible."

"Two drinks. Okay, three. But I'm not even buzzed." His dark stare unnerved her as he pulled her hips against his—and into his bulging erection.

"Brodie—"

When he stared down into her eyes that way, she couldn't formulate words. "I'm dancin' with my business partner. No harm in that." He shot a glare over her shoulder, and she didn't need to whirl to know it was directed at Wayne.

"Is that all I am to you? A business partner?" Her nipples ached painfully where they pressed against his searing chest.

He lifted a hand to her hair and moved it off her shoulder. Was it her imagination or did she detect a shudder in him? He skimmed a fingertip over her bra strap before grabbing her waist again.

The way he spread his fingers so low over her back made her instantly wet. She dragged in a deep breath to steady herself, but his scents flooded her mind and made her run hotter.

Wetter.

"Of course you're more than a business partner to me. You're Matt's little sister."

The urge to knee him in the balls was hot and bright. Her muscles leaped.

She had to get some distance between them, but the song wasn't over and he wasn't letting go. His grip was too hard, too perfect. She wanted him pinning her to the wall and fucking her slow and deep. Or dragging her up to meet his thrusts, his fist in her hair.

Biting back a moan, she darted a look at Wayne. He was too nice a guy to act like a possessive jackass, but he wasn't happy. His hands were clenched into fists at his sides and his face was shadowed with anger.

"Brodie, I'd like to end this dance now."

"I didn't get a whole song, though." He walked his fingers lower, extending them over her ass. Heat ribboned through her.

"I'm on a date. I'll see you tomorrow."

He stopped swaying, his gaze cutting her heart out. "You're having a good time with that guy?"

She hadn't spent enough time with him to know yet. "He's taking me riding after this."

"Riding?" He arched a dark brow, rendering her panties a completely soggy scrap. "I'll take you ridin', sweetheart. Even on a horse sometimes."

Oh God. His hot, dirty words spoken so low and close to her ear sent her reeling. She couldn't draw breath or even think. He had to be buzzed, but she didn't care. She wanted to throw her arms around his neck and her thighs around his hips and let him carry her to the nearest truck bed. Lay her out and make her forget her own name.

"Brodie, I think those three drinks are affecting you more than you believe."

He shook himself but she didn't see a hint of the drunkenness she was suggesting. "No, I'm just acting in a brotherly fashion. I need to know you're happy with that guy. Because last week you couldn't get away from him fast enough."

"Keep your voice down. Wayne's okay. He's really nice."

"So you're asking me to let you go so you can dance with him?"

She pushed out a sigh. She was happy right where she was. Sharing great conversation and being swirled through another ballad by the biggest, baddest cowboy in Shooters was the best way to spend an evening.

But Wayne deserved better. Besides, she'd been having a good time up until the moment she'd spied Brodie across the room.

"Yes, Brodie. I'll talk to you tomorrow."

His lips tightened briefly but he let her go with a smile. It didn't reach his eyes, but she'd made her choice and this was better. She wanted to have a good time tonight and forget about her ruined town and the family who'd been sliced apart. Wayne came without any baggage. He was genuine and...simple.

She wanted that tonight.

She gave Brodie a nod of goodbye and crossed the dance floor to take Wayne's hand. "Let's grab a drink."

Unfortunately Brodie had beaten them to the bar and was talking to a little blonde bartender who had enough flirt in her for five girls. Brodie avoided Danica's gaze as he laid down some bills and went away with a whole bottle of whiskey.

"Wait, Brodie."

He gripped the neck and strolled past her, headed for his buddies. Matt's buddies. Guys she considered family. They'd take care of the man who seemed bent on self-destruction tonight.

Wouldn't they?

Wayne passed her the light beer she'd ordered and led her to a table off the dance floor—out of Brodie's line of sight. They discussed his job and an upcoming prom he'd signed up to chaperone. She was so absorbed in thoughts of Brodie getting too drunk and losing control that she totally missed when Wayne asked her to be his date.

"Where?" she asked.

"At the prom."

Prom? Were they seventeen again? Christ, she couldn't think of a worse way to spend an evening.

"Oh. I'll think about it. I don't have much in the way of dresses."

He dropped his eyes to her chest and back up. "You'd look beautiful in a paper bag, Danica."

"Uh, thank you." What was wrong with her? Here was a man hitting all the high notes of dating etiquette—he opened doors, bought her drinks, and complimented her. But she couldn't get Brodie's dirty suggestion that she could ride something besides a horse out of her head.

"Do you still want to go riding?" Wayne was asking.

She snapped back to the present and the man before her. A good, stable man, she reminded herself again. "Yes. Let's go." She slurped another bit of beer and put her hand in Wayne's. As they left Shooters, she tried not to look around for Brodie. It had to be her imagination that she could feel his hot stare on her. Either that or she was losing it.

* * * * *

Brodie's head was as fragile as an eggshell. He raised it slowly; it felt too much to bear and he lowered it to his pillow again.

What an idiot he was. He knew lots of soldiers who'd turned to drink after realizing they didn't have a place in society. He'd vowed to never be one of them. But last night, that's exactly what he'd done. He'd convinced himself he wasn't good enough for the one woman in the bar who was worth spending time with.

After Danica had left Shooters, he'd gotten caught in an emotional tornado and drank until his world stopped spinning. But it didn't change things.

He fucking wanted Danica.

There was no denying the primal need she raised in him. And being around her made him forget he'd lost his best friend and his town. She'd given him something to look forward to every day.

Going for a second try, he lifted his head and made it to an upright position.

"Brodie?" His mother's high-pitched voice abraded his nerves, and even turning his head toward the door hurt like hell.

"Yeah, Ma." He could barely force the words past his cracked throat. His head threatened to tip off his shoulders, so he held it in place.

When she opened the door and saw his state, her lips compressed in that line of disapproval. A hundred lectures surfaced in his mind, but he couldn't locate the one she was about to give.

"Don't...say it," he choked out. "I feel bad enough."

She bustled into the room and picked up a few dirty clothes he'd scattered on the floor. He started to tell her he'd handle it—he was a grown-ass man. But he didn't have the energy.

"Your friends are on the porch waiting for you."

His heart leapt at the thought of Danica out there. "What friends?" When he stood, the world did two complete spins. His stomach lurched. For a grown-ass man, he was a dumb one. *Never again.* He and whiskey could remain friends—just not such close ones.

"The boys. Wydell, Garrett, and Boyd. Something's gone wrong and they want your advice."

Damn. "Wrong?"

He had no choice but to bend over and grab his pants. Last night, even reeling from too much alcohol, he'd had a hard-on that wouldn't go away. He vaguely remembered taking off his pants to ease the tightness around his cock. A distant memory of groaning Danica's name flooded his mind.

"They didn't tell me what's wrong. You'll have to find that out for yourself."

His mother remained tactfully turned away while he pulled on his jeans, handling himself as he would C-4. Pulling up his zipper hurt everything including his back teeth, but he managed it and the button. The belt seemed beyond him, though, and he withdrew it from his belt loops and tossed the leather onto the bed.

For a dizzying second, his mind locked on it and all he could see was Danica's bare ass hiked into the air, awaiting a spanking.

He shuddered and his head nearly fell off again. "All right. Please tell me there's coffee."

"Always." She pivoted to give him a concerned look. "Are you feeling up to this?"

"I did it to myself, Ma. I'll manage." As he passed her, he touched her arm. She leaned in and pecked his cheek, and he was consumed by guilt. He should start living up to his parents' expectations. And start enjoying being home too. While in the desert, he'd dreamed of his momma's home cooking. Yet he was still eating as if it were military rations, and she was constantly asking him if her meals were to his liking.

How to explain that he wasn't really able to enjoy anything right now? His stomach was still a ball of worry. The most solace he got was with Danica.

After grabbing a thermos of coffee, he pushed through the screen door, careful not to let it bang behind him. His buddies stood in a huddle. The minute he saw their faces, his heart squeezed hard. Painfully.

"Who?" he grated out. Suddenly he was back in combat, awaiting a name of the fallen. His heart thumped and he started counting fast.

Garrett came forward, tugging down his hat in a nervous gesture. "Nobody, Brodie." He gripped Brodie's shoulder, and it was a good thing—Brodie didn't know if he could remain standing if he heard bad news.

God, I'm shell-shocked. "Nobody's dead?"

"I wouldn't say that—"

"Wydell, stop. Let me tell him." Garrett met Brodie's stare, his jaw working.

"Is it Danica?" He couldn't breathe. For the first time in his life, he was going to let his emotions best him.

Garrett's face registered shock. "No, man. God, no. She's fine, far as I know. But it's the Popes' dog."

He needed to sit down after all. His knees buckled, and he folded, hunching into a squat, head bowed. "What the hell happened?"

Garrett bent, keeping a hand on his shoulder. This was all wrong—Brodie had held the guys together after Matt's death. Now he seemed to be unable to process the smallest upset—like the loss of a dog.

Not any old dog. His dog. Her dog. Fuck.

"We've been clearing the barn debris at my place when we don't have a job in town." Garrett's gray eyes burned into him, centering him. "We heard some whimpers."

"I thought it was a cat," Wydell offered. "But we looked closer."

"It was the Popes' dog," Garrett finished.

"Please tell me it's not Crow." Brodie's voice sounded like glass under a boot heel. He looked up at Boyd, who gave a single slow nod. Brodie grated out, "It is Crow. Fucking hell. Let's go."

Five minutes later they were bouncing up the rutted lane to Garrett's property. Partway Brodie gave up holding his head in place and let the sickness steal over him.

The house was caved in, but the family had taken up residence in a shed they'd expanded into a lean-to. His parents and younger brother were nowhere to be seen, which was good. Brodie couldn't face conversation.

He got out of the old Ford and three other doors slammed shut. Striding to the barn ruins, he prepared himself. The guys had told him the dog's whimpers had stopped before they could find a way to get him out. Apparently Crow had been sniffing around the foundation and a beam had shifted, trapping him. Crushing him.

Brodie forgot all about his throbbing temples and sour stomach as he approached the barn. By the looks of it, the structure had taken a direct hit. Wood was splintered. Hay had been forced into the wood by high winds so it looked as if it had a run-in with a porcupine.

Swallowing hard, Brodie said, "I don't see him."

"There." Boyd extended an arm.

The moment Brodie spotted the black coat, his stomach rebelled. He turned and heaved while his buddies moaned with disgust.

"You're never drinking again if you can't hold your damn stomach, Sergeant."

He swiped the back of his hands over his mouth and straightened. "Have no intention of it." How was he going to tell Danica her dog was dead while sporting a hangover? He wasn't sure he and Danica were even on friendly terms after last night.

If he could give himself a kick in his own ass, he'd do it.

"Garrett, get me some rope. I'm going in."

Within seconds he'd fashioned a harness from rope. The guys gripped the end like a tug of war team. The barn foundation wasn't deep, but he wouldn't be able to grab anything—at least nothing that wouldn't give way. So they needed to lower him the few feet, let him get to the dog, and then pull him out.

"Nice and slow, men." Garrett's tone was so reminiscent of their last mission, Brodie's head swam and his stomach clenched again.

He positioned his foot on a wobbly board. It shifted and he chose another. And another. Making slow progress toward the caved-in area where Crow lay. Brodie had to get him out. The animal was far from home.

Behind Brodie, his friends grunted directions to him. But he'd do this alone. He'd gotten Matt out too.

"Crow, old boy." Somehow the dog was all tangled up with his reunion with Danica. He could nearly feel her long legs wrapped around him as she wet his shoulder with her tears. No matter how they'd left things last night, he was there for her. They were practically family, goddammit.

"A few more feet. Can anybody see a direct path?" he called.

"Left. Left for sure. It looks safest, Brodie."

He eyed the tilted rafters. The last thing he wanted was to end up suffocating beneath a heavy beam the way Crow had.

A faint noise reached him. He stopped dead, his ears working out the sound beneath the creak of the board he was standing on.

A whimper.

"He's alive!" His heart surged. Tossing away all caution, he walked the length of the board he was standing on like a tightrope walker. When he reached the end, it tipped

139

precariously and he barely jumped to another before he got his leg broken.

One of the guys whooped. Another called for him to watch himself. The rope around his chest and upper thighs tightened as he reached the dog.

Crow lay pinned beneath a rafter and another board, but his chest was definitely moving up and down. Too fast, though. He had to get him out of there — now.

"I got ya, boy." A knot put in his chest by Matt and Danica pulled hard. He had to save the dog for her sake — and her parents'. Another blow would likely cripple Mrs. Pope.

When he unclipped a short length of rope from his belt loop, he eased into a kneeling position. Beneath the dog and the wreckage was black space. They were suspended on boards fallen and twisted, but the barn floor was a good six feet down.

Not a lot of distance to fall, but God knew what was down there to fall *on*.

Using all his strength and caution, he shifted the beam off the animal. As soon as the weight was free, the dog's chest heaved.

Crow whimpered, and Brodie made a soothing noise as he slipped the rope around Crow's body. When he was trussed like a calf in a ravine, Brodie glanced over his shoulder at his friends.

"Grab this!" He tossed. All his practice roping Danica paid off now. Garrett caught the end. They began to pull out Crow, and Brodie very carefully turned to navigate his was across the sea of wreckage to the safety of land.

"Let's pick up Danica and get the dog to the vet."

Chapter Five

When Danica spotted the blue Ford rambling up the driveway, she swiped a hand down her face. Damn, she wasn't in the mood for Matt's friends right now. She was running on little sleep and the slightest talk of her brother would spark tears.

Better that she greet the guys than her parents, though. They weren't up to it.

The car stopped in a cloud of dust. Danica pulled off her work gloves and started toward the vehicle, when the back door opened and Brodie unfolded himself.

"Danica."

Crap. She wasn't in the state of mind to discuss what had happened last night—which was nothing. They'd danced and she'd returned to her date. End of story.

Except…

"You look like shit," she said. His clothes were grubby and looked as if he'd slept in them. Dirt smudged his sharp cheekbone. In the shadows of his hat, his eyes were bloodshot. "How much did you drink?"

"Too much. Or maybe not enough since I'm not still drunk. I need you to get in the car."

"What?" She looked at Wydell's grave gaze through the window. "What's going on?"

Brodie moved a few inches so she could see inside the car. On the seat was a familiar lump of black, typically seen on the front porch directly in the way of where she wanted to step.

"Crow! Oh God, what's happened to him?"

"Get in and I'll explain. We're taking him to town. Wydell's already phoned the vet."

She dropped her gloves and rushed toward the car. As she took the seat Brodie had vacated, Garrett climbed out the other door. "I'll take over your chores. Not enough room for all of us anyway."

Tears clogged her throat as she settled a hand on her dog's side. Crow whimpered, and she snatched her fingers back.

"Thanks, Garrett." Brodie's deep voice flickered on the edge of her hearing, along with a car door closing. Her mind was too stunned to process the words. Wydell drove back down the driveway and to the main road.

Danica searched out Brodie's gaze. It almost pained her to look at him for too long. "What happened to Crow?"

"Found him in Garrett's barn, trapped. He could have internal injuries." He reached across the dog and took Danica's fingers. As his warm, callused hand closed around hers, a

144

tear trickled down her cheek. She swiped it away and refused to let another fall.

"What was he doing at the Gentrys' place?" she asked.

"Dunno." He chafed her fingers with a light caress that shouldn't have touched her so deeply. But it did. It was impossible not to compare Brodie's hands with Wayne's softer ones. Though the man was an experienced horseman, he wasn't as rugged as Brodie.

Pulling her hand from his, she stroked her dog. Crow was curled tightly, his eyes squeezed shut, and his breathing was shallow. But he was alive, which was one step toward being okay.

Neither man in the front of the car spoke. It was as if seeing Matt's dog wounded was akin to seeing the man himself.

Tears threatened, and she dragged in deep breaths to dispel them. The rest of the journey was driven in silence. As soon as they reached the veterinary hospital, Brodie hopped out and strode inside. He came back with a couple people in scrubs pushing a cart.

They got Crow out of the car and onto it, and Danica helplessly watched her family dog being rolled away.

Brodie appeared at her side, and she couldn't resist the pull of his solid arms. She leaned into him. He held her, his warm hand on her nape grounding her.

Wydell and Boyd surrounded them. "We're going to walk up to the coffee shop. Can we bring you back something?" Wydell asked.

"Bring a coupla coffees," Brodie answered in a quiet tone.

She turned her face against his chest for a moment, smelling bar food and whiskey. He hadn't even changed out of his clothes. She pushed away.

He eyed her warily. "Let's go inside. There's bound to be paperwork."

"Okay."

Once she'd filled out several forms, Brodie took the clipboard to the window. He spoke with the receptionist for a long minute before pulling his wallet from his back pocket.

She bolted to her feet. "No, Brodie. You don't have to pay."

He glanced at her. "We'll worry about it later." His tone said differently, though. The stubborn man had no intention of allowing her or her family to pay for whatever care Crow required.

She sank to the hard seat again. Her mind was spinning, and she couldn't seem to land on any one thought. As Brodie filled the chair—no, overflowed it—beside her, she folded her hands in her lap. Touching him made her synapses snap. Having him near was no good for her peace of mind.

"Glad you made it home okay last night," he said.

She shot him a look. "Meaning?"

"Why are you so touchy? I spoke plain. I didn't mean anything by it."

Fine. She'd let it go. "When will we hear about Crow?"

"They're looking at him now. They'll tell us as soon as they make some decisions."

His words fell between them. The idea of Crow needing to be put to sleep made her throat burn. Brodie rested a hand on her knee, and she briefly clasped his fingers. Touching him was too normal for her, and she didn't want him to get the wrong idea. The way he'd barged in and demanded a dance with her last night was totally cocky.

And totally hot.

"So what time did you get in this morning?" His question vibrated with insinuation. She should be pissed off. So why was she leaning toward him?

"What time did you?" she shot back.

"Too damn late." He pulled his hand off her knee and scrubbed it over his face. The rasping noise of callus on beard only spiked her awareness. While she couldn't be further from horny, she couldn't deny she wanted to climb into his lap and curl around him. To take comfort.

Would she do that with Wayne if he were here? The answer was a swift *no.* The man was nice, but...

He wasn't Brodie.

She peered at him from the corner of her eye. "You rescued Crow?"

He gave a simple nod.

"I guess I'd better thank you, then."

His mouth softened and his eyes were hot pools of melted chocolate. She wanted to dive in and do backstrokes. "No thanks needed, Danica. I'd do anything for your family."

It was on the tip of her tongue to ask, *For my family or for me?* But two vets came out of a

149

door and waved for her and Brodie to follow. Standing on wobbly legs, she sucked in a deep breath in preparation for the worst possible news.

Brodie rested his hand on her spine and led her to the door. His warmth spread through her, and she relaxed a bit. Whatever happened, she had him by her.

* * * * *

Brodie tucked Danica under his arm and handed her a wad of tissues. Her tears were unstoppable now that they'd been told Crow had soft tissue injuries that would heal in time, as well as some cracked ribs, and one had punctured his lung.

She took the whole handful of tissues and pressed them all to her nose at once. His heart surged with protectiveness and fondness as he led her into the waiting room again while they prepped Crow for surgery.

Wydell and Boyd stood as soon as they appeared. Looking anxious, Wydell held out two cups of coffee and Boyd offered a waxed bag that probably contained donuts. Brodie's stomach turned.

"Just the coffee for me. Thanks." He took his, and Danica juggled her tissues to accept her cup. Once Brodie had her seated, Boyd passed her the bag of donuts with a soft word.

She blinked at him through tear-wet lashes. "Thank you." She took out one of the glazed donuts and bit into it, sniffling as she chewed.

Seeing her eat heartened him. She'd always had a great appetite, because hell, she worked as hard as a cowboy. Watching her made him think of those women he'd taken out between tours. He'd spend a fortune on a nice meal, and they'd pick at the food.

Brodie filled in his friends on Crow's health. They discussed going back into town to start work on one of the lots, but that meant leaving Brodie and Danica without wheels. It was decided they could all take a day off.

Danica lifted the bag in offering to Brodie. "Are you going to eat this?"

"Nah." He rested a hand on his sickly stomach. "You go on."

She withdrew the second donut and bit off a huge bite. "I stress eat. I shouldn't, but they taste so good. And I only had coffee this morning. My parents…" She clamped off the sentence.

Brodie knew things weren't great at the Popes' place. And Danica was alone to deal with her parents' grief as well as her own, on top of running the ranch. He eased his arm around her shoulders and drew her close to him. Even with the chair arms between them, he was able to feel her soft curves and body heat. Right now, he'd like to curl around her. Spoon her and sleep.

She leaned her head against his and polished off her donut. When she licked each delectable fingertip, he had to straighten away from her. Either that or haul her into his lap and ravish her.

Boyd picked up a women's magazine and started reading the latest dish on celebrities. Wydell got into one of his snorting laugh fits, and Danica soon joined them with giggles.

"Are you okay?" she asked, nudging Brodie with her elbow.

"There's not enough caffeine in the world to stop my head from aching."

"We could walk down the street to the drugstore." Her eyes, so close and serious, sent a brand new wave of need though him. This had nothing to do with hormones — she was a beautiful sweetheart of a woman, and he wanted to get closer to her.

He nodded. Standing, he reached for her hand. She gave it to him, clasping fingers. His friends looked pointedly at their joined hands and said they'd wait for news on Crow. Later Brodie would need to end the rumors that would be flying about him and Danica, but right now he didn't have the energy.

Besides, her hand felt too good in his.

Outside, the sunlight pierced his skull, and he couldn't bite off his groan in time.

"Serves you right. Why'd you get so drunk?"

He couldn't tell her she was the reason. That he'd gone out of his goddamn mind seeing her leave with that schoolteacher, knowing they were going to spend the rest of the evening together. Only whiskey had been able to temporarily stop him from thinking about her being in that man's bed.

He didn't respond to her question—just opened the door of the drugstore for her. She passed through and went straight to a rack beside the counter where one-dose packets of medicine hung. She plucked off two and set them on the counter.

Arching a brow, he said, "Anything else?"

"Yes." She chose a pack of mints and added them to the pile. "For you. You smell."

The cashier eyed them with amusement.

"I suppose Wayne has minty-fresh breath? He probably smells like flowers too, not manure." He fished out his wallet and grabbed a couple bills to pay for the items.

"Leave Wayne out of this."

The cashier's head bounced back and forth between them.

"I always knew you'd choose a guy like him." He thrust the money at the cashier.

Danica's eyes widened so the irises swam in an ocean of white. "What's that supposed to mean?"

"You always picked the wimpy types."

"Whaaa—?" Her mouth hung open. But not for long. Her fury was only back-building. "He is not remotely wimpy. He's actually quite strong."

"I'm not even going to ask for examples. I don't give a damn about his attributes. Especially knowing what you two did last night."

The cashier's gaze darted back and forth as if she were watching a tennis match. Danica served him up a mouthful of rage with a side of country twang. "It's none of your business what we did or didn't do. You're nothing to me."

"Nothing?"

She faltered.

He grabbed the bag from the cashier with a nod of thanks and spun for the door, hating his head and stomach at that minute but despising his mouth more. Opening this conversation was like firing on an army when you didn't have enough ammunition.

Or in this case, enough desire to shoot more stupid, hurt words at Danica. She deserved better.

She stormed out behind him. "Damn you for that, Brodie Bell."

"You don't need to. I'm damning myself. I'm sorry."

"You should be. Matt would knock your teeth out for embarrassing me in front of that cashier."

"Yeah, he would." Maybe Brodie wished for that a little. At least he'd be able to shut up and stop himself from saying how badly he wanted Danica. Or how damn jealous he was of Wayne.

He pressed his lips together and held up a hand against further tirade. She gave an angry huff and stalked past him, walking fast down the sidewalk to the vet's office. When he entered, she was seated between Wydell and Boyd, looking at a magazine with them. But

157

the flush high on her cheeks spoke of her discomposure.

Brodie ripped open the painkiller and stomach medicine packets and chased the handful of pills with cold coffee. How to fix things with his feisty cowgirl?

His big mouth had cancelled any good deeds such as rescuing her dog or bringing Crow in for surgery. Damn, he was an idiot.

* * * * *

Danica lifted the spoon to her mouth, her attention on the TV screen. She stuffed her mouth with kids' cereal and crunched noisily. Sunday mornings were made for kicking back—after she did ranch chores, of course.

She'd cleaned the stalls and fed and watered cattle. She'd even seen to a calf that was favoring one leg. But she was happy to sit and veg for a little while.

Her dog was improving but needed another night or two in the veterinary hospital. Her parents had expressed worry, but their grief-ravaged faces hadn't changed much. Danica had assured them Crow would be fine and she'd made them a good dinner last night. Neither had eaten much, and her mother had left the table first. When she'd emerged from the bathroom some time later, her eyes had been red-rimmed.

Danica wished she could lighten their sadness but she'd heard time was key with grief. For now, she was enjoying a spot of peace and relaxation, even if it was with Bugs Bunny.

The Road Runner vanished into a cave, but Wile E. Coyote smashed his face off the rock surface. When he fell backward with birds and stars swirling around his head, a deep laugh sounded behind her.

She threw a look over her shoulder and nearly choked on her cereal. Brodie stood there, thumb hooked in his belt buckle, a crooked smile painted on his handsome features.

He moved into the living room. "You got more cereal?"

"In the kitchen."

He turned and walked into the kitchen. She went dead still. What was he doing here? Besides going after a bowl of cereal.

A minute later he returned carrying a brimming bowl. When he settled beside her on the couch, his thigh so close she felt his scorching heat, he gestured at the TV with his spoon.

"Like old times. Cartoons and cereal."

Her heart gave a strange flip-flop. He was right—she, Matt, and Brodie had spent countless mornings this way.

They munched in silence while the Road Runner bested the coyote. After Brodie had gulped down half his bowl, he dropped his spoon into it and sat back. His big legs splayed naturally and he cradled the bowl in one broad palm.

She set her bowl on the coffee table and turned to him. "Everything okay?"

When he met her gaze full force, she forgot about their argument. Suddenly she only remembered the good he'd done—on the ranch, for her dog. He'd even been helping some of the few families in town by dropping off eggs from their chickens.

"Everything's fine." His eyes practically smoldered. "Just came by to do chores, but you have it covered."

"Yeah. Do you want to work on the enclosure?"

"Figured we would." He didn't look ready to budge.

"Okay, well, finish your cereal and we'll get to it." She started to stand, but he caught her wrist. His longer fingers encircled her flesh, searing places that had nothing to do with her arm. "Brodie?"

"Are we okay, Danica? Because I can't stand it if we're not okay." The gravel in his voice abraded her control. He looked like a lost puppy with those deep brown eyes and the cute way his eyebrows furrowed.

"We're okay, Brodie."

He reeled her in until she had no choice but to sit beside him again. This time their thighs touched. Even with layers between them, she knew his worn denim was supersoft, making her fingers twitch to feel more.

"I'm sorry for the way I acted at Shooters."

"Okaaaay." Her warm, fuzzy feeling about him started to vanish like a morning fog under the sun.

"And for the drugstore incident."

"Is this the point in the conversation where you pinch me and call me Easter?"

His gaze raked over her face, raising a shiver in her. "No, sweetheart. I truly am sorry. Forgive me?"

The moment was too heavy. Feeling an intense need to lighten it, she said, "Only if you finish your cereal. It's your favorite."

A crooked smile broke over his face. "You remember."

"Yeah, because it's my favorite too."

He released her wrist and lifted his hand toward her face. For two long heartbeats it hovered a scant inch from her cheek before he dropped it. "I'm not very hungry lately. I think I am but after a few bites... Let's see if this cereal's the pigs' favorite too."

With that, he stood and strode from the room, leaving her to blink after him. What was that near-caress of his hand near her cheek? And what was bothering him so much that it was affecting his appetite?

The man was driving her crazy. And damn if she didn't like it.

* * * * *

Danica seated her mare with such skill and pride that Brodie could hardly look away from her. The sun seemed to have come out just to kiss her golden-tan flesh. She rode before him, issuing orders to the two dogs running between them and the herd.

Since barreling into Los Vista weeks ago, prepared to take on civilian life with gusto, he'd lost a little of his momentum. There was no reason for it—he and Danica had achieved so much with the ranches already. Soon they would finish the enclosure that would fuse their ranches as one.

Danica's long, dark ponytail bounced on her spine, which was covered in plaid fabric of pinks and pale oranges. Sunset colors. Too well he could imagine running his hands over that warm fabric and drawing it off her arms. Leaning in to kiss and nibble her throat, collarbones. Breasts.

Shuddering, he pushed his horse to catch up with hers. Today she rode a nice, quiet animal. It suited her. His own horse was one he hadn't ridden much before. He found it a bit ornery, but they were getting along fine.

When he neared Danica, her horse's ears perked up. It tossed its head.

Danica glanced around and saw Brodie. "What are you doing? My horse doesn't like it."

"Just ridin' alongside you."

Her horse snorted and shied away. Danica gave the mare enough lead to put her in her comfort zone again. But Brodie's horse wouldn't have it—the gelding angled right for the mare.

"What the hell, Brodie?" Danica's animal reared. A squeak left her as her world upended.

"Danica!" His heart slammed against his rib cage seeing her dangling in the saddle. His sharp cry brought his horse up. Her mare's hooves hit the ground. The dogs scattered.

Danica quickly shifted herself into a solid position in the saddle, and she righted her hat. Beneath it, her eyes were bright with anger. "My horse hates yours. Keep it away from her."

"This isn't my fault. How was I supposed to know they don't get along?"

"Considering you and I don't get along—"

"What the hell are you talking about, woman? We get along fine."

"Unless I do something you have no control over."

He eased his horse as close as possible without pissing off her mare. Never again did

Brodie want to see her clinging to the saddle to keep from falling and being trampled. His pulse was still racing and he wanted to draw her into his arms just to make sure she was okay.

"I have no idea what you're talking about, Danica."

She stretched a hand before her, indicating the rolling fields of golden grasses. "Out here we have few problems."

"What about in your living room watching cartoons this morning?"

She didn't reply, her head held high as if she were scanning the horizon for an answer she didn't have.

Brodie rode closer, and her mare's ears stiffened. Danica shot him a scowl, but he wasn't moving away until she answered him. "We're friends. Always have been," he said.

"I never said we weren't."

"But you're implying that I'm controlling and if I don't get my own way, I'm difficult to get along with."

She laughed, a buttery sound that coated his insides. A man could accept high cholesterol if he feasted on that every day. "You don't want to get me started on what happened at Shooters or the drugstore."

"No, I don't. But we obviously aren't working past it until we clear the air. So lay it out for me, darlin'."

When she threw him a glare, his heart flexed. She was stunning, especially when angry. He wanted to rile her until she snapped. Then he'd pin her arms above her head and kiss the cuss words off her pretty little pout. His cock stirred.

"I don't want to get into it with you, Brodie."

"You're holding a grudge. You never were a grudge holder."

"No? What about that time you told the guys you'd rather kiss your horse than me? I didn't talk to you for weeks."

He burst out laughing, too late realizing it was the wrong reaction. Her gaze trained on him like guns on an enemy. "It's funny—"

"Funny? It's not remotely funny."

"You cut me off. I meant it's funny you mention it because I was thinking about it a few days back."

His horse edged too close. The mare swung her head around, teeth flashing. Thankfully neither animal got spooked, and Brodie was able to catch hold of Danica's ponytail. The length slid through his palm like warm silk, and suddenly his jeans were excruciatingly tight.

"Get your horse away from mine."

"Danica, look at me." His command brought her head around. Their gazes locked and her lips fell open at whatever she saw on his face. He dropped his gaze to her mouth. "I don't prefer my horse now."

She twisted away. "But you did then. You're not forgiven." Her tone suggested otherwise.

They swayed in their saddles, cattle lowing around them. One of the dogs zipped past. And Brodie ached to pull Danica off her horse and into his lap.

She flicked her head, and her ponytail slipped from his hand. She spurred her mare into a trot and left him to stare at her back— and her supple behind bouncing up and down. Jesus, she was going to kill him. But she was right in one way—he was used to being in control but with her he was on a landslide.

He wasn't giving up. He kicked his horse into gear. In seconds they were astride again. He caught Danica's quiet groan as he appeared beside her.

"I don't like the schoolteacher," he said quietly.

Her head whipped around. "Why the hell not? You know what? It doesn't matter. You don't get a say."

"The first time I saw the guy, you practically jumped into my truck and begged me to take you far away from him."

"I didn't put it that way."

"You didn't want to spend time with the man. What changed?"

"I realized I don't have a reason not to see him. He's a nice guy. A good guy."

"He's not for you."

That look—the Pope look—Matt had given him the same expression countless times in battle. It was Matt's poker face. Matt couldn't have displayed his true feelings or he'd risk alarming the platoon. Danica didn't feel she could either, and that hurt.

Brodie held up a hand. "Look, you're not going to convince me that you're actually interested in this guy."

"What if I told you I went to bed with him Friday night?"

His ab muscles clenched as he stared at her. "Did you?"

When she didn't answer, he caught her around the waist and yanked her right out of the saddle.

She cried out, kicking, but he settled her across his lap. Her mare made a run for it.

"My horse!"

"Let her go. But you aren't getting away." *Not this time.*

"I'm not a young girl anymore, Brodie." She moved as if to jump down, but he secured her. Wicked curves were pinned to his body in all the right places. Jesus, he was losing his mind. No, she was stealing it.

"I know you're not a kid, darlin'."

"Stop calling me that." Her chest rose and fell, and her eyes darkened.

172

Before he could figure out what he was doing, he lowered his head. "Okay, I won't. Squirt." He claimed her mouth.

* * * * *

The first brush of Brodie's lips against hers dragged a ragged moan from her throat. She felt as though she was free-falling, but she was tightly locked in Brodie's arms. His flavors flooded her mind, and she parted her lips on a gasp.

He took immediate advantage, thrusting his tongue into her mouth. Forcing her to open wider for his invasion. With a shudder of desire, she threw her arms around him and dragged him closer.

Angling his head, he swept the interior of her mouth, his hot tongue tasting of pure, raw need. Her breasts ached and her nipples throbbed where they were pressed against his chest. Never in her life had she been kissed while on horseback. Or kissed like this.

She dug her nails into his shoulders as she touched her tongue to his. Tasting, taking, and giving. She really must have pushed him far enough that he no longer saw her as Matt's kid sister. *Took him long enough.*

As she tangled her tongue around his, she let her fingers trail up his throat. Her fingertips brushed the rough stubble on his jaw, and she stroked it. Again and again. Burning to feel that prickle all over her bare body.

He tore his mouth free and glared down at her. "Did you sleep with him Friday night?"

She drew him down until their noses bumped. "No." Her whisper was swallowed by his possessive kiss. The rumbled growl ignited her. She closed her eyes and let him control her. She could get used to this free-falling feeling.

He hauled her higher on his lap so her hip pressed against his rigid cock. Her heart pounded as she realized just how far this could go between them. And why not? She was sick of denying he was perfect for her.

He tore from the kiss again and flipped her upright to straddle the horse. Brodie groaned as her ass ground against his erection. "This isn't over. Not by a long shot." His rough words caressed her neck, prickling her skin.

She looked down at his gloved fists with reins looped around them and imagined his touch all over her body. She wiggled backward.

A growl burst from him. "I can't keep my hands off you."

"I don't want you to try."

He urged his horse along the fence. Placing his mouth to Danica's ear, he grated out, "Slide off, cowgirl. Nice and slow."

Oh God. What did he want from her? She dragged in a deep breath and slid out of the saddle. Her boots barely touched down before

Brodie was on her. Crushing her to his chest, his mouth bruising.

She kissed back with everything inside her. His tongue seemed to be attached by invisible thread to her pussy and nipples. Cupping her face, he tipped her head back to receive him. Long, sweeping passes of his tongue as if he truly couldn't get enough.

She couldn't, that was certain. She stroked his spine, damp with perspiration, down to his steely buns. Hitching him against her drew a lusty moan from each of them.

"You need more from a man than that teacher can give." His eyes were nearly black. She swore she could feel his cock throbbing against the V of her legs.

Wiggling closer, she leaned onto tiptoe to put Brodie right where she wanted him. "You think so?"

"I know." That command in his tone stole her last thread of self-control. When he tugged off his leather gloves, her heart began to pound. She captured his mouth and fumbled with his shirt buttons. With every inch of flesh she bared, her pussy pulsated. When she reached his belt buckle, he stayed her, his fingers locked around her wrists.

As she saw the decision in his eyes, her heart turned over and did a happy dance.

He unbuttoned her top with record speed, tearing off one of the buttons in the process. It zinged through the high grass, lost forever. She didn't care. She bowed her back to get closer to his burning touch.

Popping her breasts from her bra cups, he groaned. The vibration zipped through her senses. Cradling one breast in her palm, she lifted it to his mouth in offering.

As his lips closed around the bud, her eyes rolled back in her head. This was what she was missing with Wayne—the passion. Unadulterated need. All the Mr. Nice Guys in the world were worth nothing without it.

She gasped as Brodie sucked her into his mouth. His tongue circled her nipple. His fingers worked her other breast, kneading and pinching the tip until she made unearthly noises. Then he shifted to her other breast.

For long minutes he worked her into a frenzy under the hot Texas sun. When she couldn't hold still, he whipped off his shirt and dropped it to the ground. "Lie down on that."

Heart tripping, she obeyed. His tone commanded her senses. Men had followed this man in battle. She could see why.

He followed her down, covering her with his bare chest. The instant his hot flesh met hers, they both stopped dead. Brodie buried his face against her neck, breathing hard. She cradled his nape, praying he wouldn't stop now.

"Danica...sweet Jesus." He raked his five o'clock shadow over her throat, up her jaw, and kissed her with a violence that spurred her to a higher plane of need.

She hooked her leg around his back, drawing his cock against her pussy.

"Fuck, I can't. I can't." His chant came time and again as he kissed between her breasts, down to her waistband. In seconds he had her jeans wiggled down her hips and her pussy exposed.

"Holy hell," he ground out as he looked at her smooth mound. Then he dipped his head and delivered a lick right over her swollen clit.

* * * * *

Dark, erotic flavors hit Brodie's taste buds, and he was helpless to resist. He buried his tongue deeper, gliding it down her sweet slit right to her core. Her jeans weren't down far enough, but he could remedy that.

As he tasted her slick need, he bared her further. With his fingers splayed on her inner thighs, he opened her to him. When he dunked

179

his tongue deep into her pussy, she threw her head back and released a throaty scream.

The sound burrowed into his mind, something to replay later when he'd found his damned mind again.

Zigzagging his tongue down her pussy lips, he felt her tension in the quiver of her thighs. He probed her opening. She groaned. And he eased inside. Fuck, he was going to come just by tasting her. She was so damn sweet and needy.

And he was an idiot. While kissing down her body, he'd realized his wallet lay at home on his dresser. Which meant no condom.

Probably just as well—he shouldn't be touching her at all. But he couldn't stop this galloping horse either.

He withdrew his tongue and flicked light caresses up to her clit. She grappled at his hair, and he found his hat was gone, lost in the grass. He opened his mouth wide and covered her whole pussy in one big bite. Sucking lightly, flicking his tongue. Driving her crazy.

"Brodie. God, yessss." She bucked into his tongue.

Stealing a peek at her face only threatened to undo him again. Her blissed-out expression would haunt him as much as her begging tone. Her thighs shook and her belly dipped. Ragged breaths left her.

He painted her clit with slow strokes of his tongue. With each pass, her nipple hardened. When he felt the first contraction of her pussy, he couldn't stop himself—he thrust a finger deep.

She shook harder, pulling his hair, grinding against his lips and finger and tongue.

And came with a soul-shuddering cry. He lapped her faster, taking her higher and wishing it were more. Wishing he could shove inside her still-pulsating body.

"More. More." Her voice was strained. He looked up her body and met her blurred-eyed gaze. He pumped his finger into her sweet heat once more. Throwing her head back, she cried out.

Fuck, why did she need to be so perfect? He wanted her unlike any woman he'd ever had. His balls ached and his cock bulged against his fly, demanding exit. But if he took his dick out of his pants, he couldn't hold himself back. He'd want to sink into her tight, lush body over and over.

Without a condom, that wasn't happening.

He had to stop now. Eating out your buddy's sister was better behavior that full-on sex, right?

In the back of his mind, Matt was already telling him off. He was supposed to protect her, not ravish her in the damn pasture. And all because of his stupid need to possess. To lock her up and keep her away from the schoolteacher.

He wasn't going to let her give herself less than full value. She deserved the kind of man who would put a grin on her face and a sway in her step. In the recesses of his mind, his inner alpha was roaring victory right now. But this was temporary. She wouldn't be happy with a man like him for long.

Matt was probably seething down from heaven, organizing a bus to come through town so he could throw Brodie under the wheels.

Pushing away, he got to his knees. Danica lay sprawled in the grass, her breasts thrust upward, her belly ring glinting in the sun. A lazy smile stretched her lips, and his heart tugged — hard.

He cloaked her with his body, allowing himself the pleasure of skin on skin. When he kissed her, damn it if she didn't swirl her tongue over his lips, moaning as she obviously tasted herself.

He had barely uncovered her inner wildcat. He wanted more — now.

It took everything in him to withdraw from her. But he pushed away and got to his feet. He had to get some distance or lose it. "I'm sorry, Squirt."

Her eyes cleared, the sexual haze gone, and he instantly regretted his words. "Don't fucking call me that."

One of the worst moments of his life was seeing her grasp the open sides of her top over her breasts as if with embarrassment. She buttoned two buttons then dragged her jeans and panties into place. When she stood, she presented her back. Seconds later, she twisted to face him. All those curves were tucked away again.

His heart beat a tempo of remorse. "I shouldn't have touched you."

For a heart-rending minute she gave him a cold stare.

He reached toward her, but she recoiled. "Look, I got carried away. I can't do this with you, Danica."

"Fuck you, Brodie." She stuck two fingers into her mouth and issued a piercing whistle. Her mare responded by trotting to her. Without a backward glance, Danica swung into the saddle and rode off, leaving him alone with only the flavors of her sweet release on his lips.

He bent and scooped up her cowgirl hat, which had fallen off in the throes of their passion. *Dammit.* He may know how to handle an enemy, but he was sure fucking up the way he dealt with his loved ones.

Chapter Six

As kids, Danica and Matt had built a treehouse. She'd borne blisters on her fingers for a week from hammering before Matt had finally insisted she wear gloves. She couldn't say she was a huge help, and the other guys had pitched in to finish.

But she'd put the homey touches on it. When she'd dragged a cooler and ice all the way up there, the boys had laughed at her. Until she'd produced a plastic jug of sweet tea and dispensed the cool drink in tiny paper cups.

She looked around the old structure, surprised it was still sturdy enough to hold her weight. Birds flitted by the window cut into the side. When she moved closer to watch their antics in the branches, she caught a glimpse of silver.

Reaching down, she put a finger over the chain and tugged. The chain slid across the floor, followed by the silver tags she never wanted to see again.

Oh God. Tears burst from her as she folded Matt's dog tags in her palm. The walls seemed to close around her. She couldn't breathe.

She bolted upright in bed, gasping. Her chest heaved and her face was wet with the tears she'd shed in her dream. She opened her palms, but they were empty. She dropped her head to her knees and focused on breathing slow and deep. But the tangled sheets were too hot, the walls of her room too constricting.

What she needed was a breath of cool night air.

She got out of bed and in the blue light cast by the moon, she located some jeans and a hoodie. Creeping out of the house in the wee hours of the morning was much easier as an adult. She made it onto the front porch, where she paused to sit and put on her boots.

Then she was walking, crossing the field that seemed to be alive with moonlight and shadows. Her family's land had a little bit of everything—rolling fields, a valley with a creek that sometimes flooded its banks in a really wet season, and a small wood that sat between their land and the Bells'.

The tornado had left all untouched, but she hadn't visited the woods since that fateful storm. Maybe the treehouse hadn't survived the high winds. Part of her hoped it hadn't.

When she first stepped into the tree line, her heart lodged in her throat. So many good memories of her brother here. Of all of them—talking and bickering. Playing cards. Cheating at cards. She stifled a teary sound when she thought about how much Matt had let her get away with.

Damn, she missed him.

As she navigated the path, she searched the treetops for the familiar walls. When the square edge came into view, she quickened her pace. A rope ladder dangled to the ground, but she wasn't about to trust a rope that had been in the elements for fifteen years. She hitched her foot on a branch and began pulling herself up.

The trapdoor was slightly ajar. She pictured a family of raccoons living up there, and stopped.

Two heartbeats passed. The branch holding her weight protested with a *crack*.

A hand appeared in the opening. Her heart squeezed so hard she thought she might be dying. A strangled cry left her as the second hand appeared, followed by a face. She let go of the branch she was holding and started to slip.

"Danica. Jesus Christ." Brodie's rough voice confused her further, and she twisted to look at the ground for the source.

But strong hands closed around her wrists and she was hauled up over the lip of the trapdoor. She sprawled over him, sending them both toppling backward into what would have been considered both living room and kitchen back in the old days.

"Are you...real?" Her own words sounded so childish, a wave of heat washed her cheeks. Thank God it was too dark for him to see and tease her.

She shook herself. Who cared? Sticks and stones didn't hurt her anymore.

He was breathing hard, and other things were stirring...below. She tried to lever herself away and a broad palm cupped her cheek. Warmth spread over her skin and traveled like wildfire along the rest of her body. Unable to help herself, she leaned into his touch.

"What are you doing here?" His voice was hoarse.

"I couldn't sleep."

"Me neither. Guess Matt called us to a meeting." The strange echo in his voice raised a shiver in her. He gathered her closer, hauling her completely atop him. They were nearly matched in height, but he made her feel so fragile, especially when he traced a path down her spine to the small of her back. His big fingertips weighted her—but to a dream world or reality?

"Brodie," she whispered.

She heard him swallow. He cleared his throat with the ripping sound of paper. In the dimness, his eyes glittered black. "I can't sleep, Danica. I've used the sides of Afghan buildings as pillows and slept soundly, but now that I have my bed I'm wide awake. And I can't eat. Momma's biscuits are dry and I can't choke them down. My favorite cereal..."

She found the line of his jaw in the darkness, running her thumb along the squared bone. "It's okay, Brodie. You're not alone."

With another rough noise, he snapped his arms around her, crushing her. The hard planes of his body comforted unlike anything had in a long time. She bit back her own emotion and just offered herself. He held her tightly for long minutes. His lips traveled over her hair.

What had happened between them in the field had been about lust. This was different. Something deep and primal was driving him to take comfort, even if it was from Matt's kid sister.

Unable to help herself, she skimmed her lips across the place she'd just touched, burning at the feel of his stiff beard beneath her lips. His body seemed to hum. Solid hips cradled hers, and his cock was steel against her pussy. He wasn't immune to her. Not at all.

His body recognized her as a grown woman.

Kissing up his chin, gunning for his hard lips, she watched his eyelids flicker. As she reached his lower lip, he closed his eyes. She nibbled.

And he turned into her kiss with a fierce possession that sucked a gasp from her. He gripped her ass and pulled her hips into his even as he rolled to meet her. When his stiff cock dug into the seam of her jeans, she released a rough cry.

"Danica, Jesus, I can't. I can't."

"You said that before. There's nothing stopping us."

He flicked his tongue over hers, towing her into a warm, mindless place where she ran on pure instinct. She needed this man. They needed each other.

Suddenly, he moved her away from him, panting hard. She found herself on cold wood, too far from the burning man she wanted so badly.

When he pushed into a sitting position, knees drawn up and head bowed, her heart gave a small pang. She rarely saw the despondent Brodie—this man was a soldier who'd seen and done horrific things. He'd seen his best friend killed.

She scooted into a sitting position too and pressed her back against the wall while she let her hormones cool. Even in her dream, she hadn't realized how tiny this place was. Or maybe it was because Brodie took up so much room.

"I'm sorry," she said softly.

He barked a humorless laugh. "Why, darlin'? It's all my fault."

"No. And I didn't come here for this. I came because I couldn't sleep. I dreamed about Matt…"

She couldn't see his face but heard his rough breathing. Putting her brother's name out there between them was a risk. Part of her wanted Brodie to only see her, not her brother. But she wasn't so man-hungry right now. She only wished to ease her friend.

Reaching across the shadows, she found his knee. When she clamped her fingers around the hard bone, she felt him shift, relaxing slightly into her touch, though his voice sounded strangled. "I can't sleep. Can't eat. I'm fucking up this living thing, Danica."

Her heart bled for the pain in his voice. "That's not how I see it. I see a man who is helping both our families. Even the townspeople see what we're doing up here and are inspired. They're starting to see they can recover and maybe rebuild."

"We're not doing enough. This town's all I've got now."

Not all you've got. Just open your eyes, Brodie.

Swallowing her personal needs, she said, "Then we'll do more. We'll hold a town meeting. Just don't shut me out. Please, Brodie."

He covered her hand over his knee and squeezed. When he released her fingers, she felt the change in him. "I'm too screwed up for you, Danica." He shuffled to the trapdoor. Desperation hit her as he dropped out of sight.

For a long time after she heard his footsteps moving away from the treehouse, she huddled against the wall, aching. She'd come here to get away from a ghost and had ended up more haunted.

* * * * *

Driving into the barren town was as depressing as hell. No businesses, no kids playing or riding bikes. Hell, he didn't even see a squirrel. He didn't see any way for the town to return to what it once was.

When Brodie spotted Danica's truck parked at the grouping of tents where Pastor Kent and his family were living, he braked. Several tents obviously blocked a fire—smoke billowed into the sky.

Without a thought he got out of the truck and began walking toward the tents. Halfway there he heard children. And hammering.

Quickening his pace, he rounded two tents to find the source of the noise. Five children ranging from ten to infancy were gathered around a fire. Mrs. Kent was bent over the flames, turning hot dogs and hamburgers while the pastor and Brodie's friends were busy laying out a framework on the ground.

Danica was nowhere to be seen.

"Brodie."

He spun at her rich, sultry drawl. He felt his eyes bulge at the sight of her cutoff shorts that featured her muscled, tanned thighs. And her white tank top was…well, he had to look away.

"Welcome, Brodie," Pastor Kent said.

He turned at the pastor's greeting. A hand was thrust out for him to shake, and Brodie looked into the man's smiling face. The darkness from the previous night fled his mind.

"Hello, Pastor. What's going on here?"

"Well, my children are fractious, as you can imagine. There's only so much homeschool they can stand before they get restless." He swept a hand across the flattened landscape. "This isn't much by way of distraction, so your friends have agreed to help me with a little building project."

Danica brushed past Brodie, hips swaying, hair long and loose on her spine. He could nearly feel her atop him again. And her sweet, plump pussy lips beneath his tongue.

"What kind of project?" He glanced away from Danica to Garrett, Wydell, and Boyd hammering and sawing some four-by-fours.

"A playground. Would you be willing to help?"

Brodie blinked. Nothing left of Los Vista. No school playground, park, or even a tire swing. It seemed fitting that one of the first structures to be built was for the entertainment of the next generation.

He smiled. "Of course. I've got a toolbox in the back of my truck. I'll get my hammer." Feeling lighter, he moved past a few toys strewn on the ground along with a bushel of clothes. The family was living in tents and making the most of it, even thriving in spirit. He felt his own soar.

When he returned to the site, Danica met his gaze. "Will you eat, Brodie?" She held a thick hamburger on a bun with lettuce and tomato. His stomach cramped.

"Yes. Thank you. And thank *you*, Mrs. Kent."

She looked up from feeding the baby with a smile and nod. Brodie walked up to his friends. The guys stood with the pastor eating and drinking. At his approach, they made space for him in their circle.

Danica joined them a minute later, mouth bulging with a hot dog. A bit of ketchup lingered at the corner of her lips, but she chewed and swallowed before swiping her tongue over it.

His gut clenched with need. Today he had his wallet, and a condom was handily tucked in the folds.

A child ran through the group, zigzagging away from his pursuer. High-pitched cries filled the air. Then Danica's voice as she made a suggestion about the playground design.

Plans were spread on the ground along with plastic bags filled with bolts and nails. A prepackaged kit purchased from a building center. The quickest means to the end result and happy children.

Maybe this was the way to rebuild…

Brodie's train of thought derailed as Danica laughed. Brodie felt as though an electric current ran through his body. His jaw twinged, and he realized he was smiling wide too.

At least until she playfully smacked Garrett in the arm. Then Brodie wanted to growl and bare his fangs like the tattoo on his arm. He watched them from beneath the brim of his hat, his appetite gone. He set his plate aside and moved toward two of the Kent children, who were red-faced from arguing.

"I get the first swing."

"No, you don't. I'm older."

"Papa says—"

Seeing the situation escalating, Brodie squatted between the kids and rested a hand on each sturdy shoulder. "Now, it looks as if there are two swings and plenty of other things to play on. You don't need to fight."

They stared at him. "Hallie gets the first swing. She's only two. We have to share with her first. It's the rules," the younger of the two said, pointing to the little blonde girl who was playing with a dirty-faced doll.

"Then you have to follow rules. But one of you can be the first to push her."

Two nods of agreement. From the corner of his eye, he saw Danica drifting closer.

"I get to push her first!"

"No, I do!"

"Why don't we flip a coin for it?" He fished in his pocket and produced a tarnished nickel. Holding it up for the youngsters, he showed them both sides. "One of you picks heads. Another tails. Whichever lands facing up wins. And that means you can't argue anymore, all right?"

Twin nods.

Danica's body heat engulfed Brodie's side where he squatted. He had to brace his muscles to keep from leaning against her strong, warm thigh. Somehow he managed to toss the coin and catch it. When he opened his palm, the kids crowded close to see.

"Heads! I get to push Hallie first."

The other child screwed up her features as if ready to scream like an air raid siren. "That means you get to swing after Hallie. Then you've gotta take turns with your brother, okay?"

Her pouting lip sucked back in and a reluctant smile spread over her features. "Okay."

At that moment, their mother called them both to eat at a picnic table. Leaving him alone with Danica.

"Nice negotiations, Sergeant."

His stomach twisted at her form of address but he smiled at her. "An argument's no good on an empty stomach."

"Is that your excuse?" She twitched her head toward his abandoned hamburger.

"I'll get back to it in a minute."

She didn't even respond to his lie, and for that he was grateful. He was mighty embarrassed about the things he'd admitted to her in the dark of the treehouse. That he couldn't eat or sleep? Hell, he might as well tell her that his guts were knotted from echoes of gunfire in his memory. And from the sound of Matt's sharp intake of breath before he'd fallen.

He shook himself, but Danica was looking at him too closely. She knew.

"Are we ready to get back to work?" Wydell stood and tucked his hammer into his tool belt. A noise of agreement ran through the group, and for the next few hours they ignored the hot sun and focused on the grins of the Kent children.

Yes, this was the town he remembered. The one he loved and couldn't wait to resurrect. How was still a huge question mark in his mind, but the moment little Hallie was settled on the swing with her brother pushing her, Brodie's hopes rocketed.

Maybe he and his friends could do something to restore dreams for other people in the community. Even those not living here right now. Yes, there were things to do outside of the ranch.

Danica strutted by with the baby in the crook of her arm. Brodie watched the pretty picture with a tight throat—and tighter jeans. Whatever they did to help, he prayed she wore those shorty shorts.

* * * * *

With the heat of the bonfire projecting over Danica's bare legs and arms, she was plenty warm. In fact, she was too hot. Brodie was seated across the fire from her, his gaze riveting her to the wooden bench she was sitting on.

Whatever was happening between them couldn't all be in her head, could it? He'd touched her. Kissed her. The way his gaze latched onto her thighs wasn't her imagination. He'd been looking at her all day.

She made a mental note to wear every pair of cutoffs in her closet. She hid a smile. *Whatever gets the job done.*

Being close to Brodie only solidified her belief that he was the man she'd been waiting for. Today his smarts and the humor she'd missed so much had surfaced, and he'd lost a little of his pinched expression. He still hadn't eaten as many calories as a man of his size should, but Los Vista wasn't built in a day. She'd take the blessings as they came.

"Are you cold, Danica? I've got a jacket in the truck." Garrett leaned near, and Brodie's eyes narrowed.

She looked away from the man she couldn't get out of her thoughts and thanked Garrett for looking out for her, but she didn't need a jacket. She was fine right there—in front of the dancing flames. She didn't say Brodie's stare was keeping her far warmer.

She tipped her head to the sky, watching sparks dancing upward. She followed their paths all the way up until they burnt out. She focused on the velvety blanket of sky and twinkling stars.

For the first time in forever, a strange contentment stole over her. It might have to do with two hot dogs in her belly along with a toasted marshmallow, but she didn't think so. Since the storm, this was her first joining with townspeople. When she was growing up, the camaraderie in Los Vista had been taken for granted by all. But after the storms and then Matt's death... Well, she felt almost normal right now.

In the back of her mind she knew she should get back home, but her father had handled chores. Besides, it was nice to be part of something that was the dead opposite of her home life.

Two of the guys joked back and forth, and a child remarked, which made everyone laugh. Danica stopped looking at the stars and met Brodie's gaze.

It was bright, hotter than the fire between them. As they stared at each other, the group discussed the whereabouts of some of the Los Vista families and what would bring them home.

When Brodie added his deep drawl, all the hairs on Danica's body stood on end, and it had nothing to do with being chilled.

"If people aren't living here, there's little need for businesses to return. We need to bring people back with the promise of shops and gas stations." He didn't look away from her.

Suddenly she had the urge to stretch like a cat, to run her hands over her body and arch under the caress of his eyes. That one orgasm he'd given her hadn't been nearly enough.

"The question is how, Brodie. I believe most people want to come home. They just don't know where to begin," one of the guys said.

"We need some cash flow first. Construct a few homes, sell them, and then put any profits into building more houses and office buildings. In time, I think we can be a town again." The conviction in his voice fueled the fires of his friends and the pastor and his wife. They all started throwing out ideas until they'd built spires and castles for all the Los Vista families.

Their enthusiasm was contagious. Danica didn't have much to add because she was too busy basking in the sound of hope. They might as well be listening to a Sunday sermon from the pastor. Brodie's voice carried a fervor that was almost religious.

"How do we bring this all about?" the pastor was asking, his own tone resonating through the group.

Danica stood. "We can visit our friends in the next towns and speak with them. We have to spread this excitement."

Brodie's stare traveled from her face over her body. When it ticked back up, she gave him a slow smile. Then she turned from the fire and sauntered away. If luck was on her side, he'd follow.

Chapter Seven

Brodie was on his feet before he could think. Moving toward Danica as if she held an invisible line and he'd been hooked. Sweet Jesus, he had. Every look and touch had been driving him crazy.

Her long legs had carried her to her truck already. Jogging, he caught up with her. As she opened her door, she glanced at him. It was too dark to make out her expression, but he was pretty damn good at reading her body language.

"Wait." He grabbed her hip and spun her away from the open door and into his arms. Walking her backward until her spine was against the truck, he stopped resisting his urges and threaded his fingers into her mass of thick hair.

"Something you needed, Brodie?"

"Yeah, this." He crushed his mouth over hers at the moment he cupped her breast. She made the sweetest fucking noise he'd ever heard and arched against him.

As he plundered her mouth, Matt's voice in his head became quieter and quieter, replaced by the one telling Brodie what Danica wanted—needed. In a flash he had his hand inside her top, plucking at her nipple. It beaded into a delicious gumdrop he was powerless to resist.

Lowering his head, he swiped the tip with his tongue, wetting her top. Once, twice, he licked her.

"Brodie, you'd better not say you can't this time. I need you."

A full-body shudder gripped him even as his balls clenched. "No, not this time. Get in the truck."

Her chest heaved but she didn't budge. "No."

He did a double take. "Did you just tell me no?"

Damn she was beautiful when she was uncertain. Her eyes darted and she wet her lips. "If you get a chance to think, you'll stop again. I'll end up home alone and fingering myself."

A growl escaped him. "That picture in my head is going to kill me. But I have no intention of letting that happen, gorgeous. If anybody is touching this pussy, it's me. Get in the truck."

He led her around to the passenger's side and put her inside. Then he got behind the wheel and found her keys dangling from the ignition. He guessed there was nobody left in town to steal it. When he started the engine and drove a short distance away to a dirt road, he shot her a sidelong look. She was right to be nervous about him cooling enough to think. Without his hands on her, Matt's voice was too loud. And it was easy to remember all the reasons he should keep his distance. He parked the truck, keeping his hands on the steering wheel to stop himself from grabbing her and doing the dirty things revolving in his head. As if realizing his mind was already working overtime, she angled her body his direction and pulled off her top. Her tits were ripe peaches spilling from the confines of her lacy bra.

His cock grew to its full length in a blink. His eyelids drooped as he looked her over. "You like touching yourself, darlin'?"

"I prefer you touching me."

He took the truck out of park and started driving again. Wanting distance and darkness in order to ravish her. "Soon enough I'll have my hands, lips and tongue all over your body. I've gotta keep my eyes on this deserted road.

But I want you to take off your bra and show me how you like your pretty breasts touched."

Why wasn't this happening during the day? He ached to see better as she filled her palms with her round breasts, her thumbs working back and forth over the straining tips. Her hair tumbled forward, and he reached across to ease it over her shoulder.

Through the darkness, her eyes burned.

"Tell me how you finger yourself, Danica."

Her breathing grew uneven. "I stretch out on my bed."

"Naked?" His tone was ragged, and in the back of his mind he realized just how out of control he was. But he wasn't about to stop now. He needed this woman on a basic level, like air or water.

"Yes, nude." She trailed her fingers around each pouty nipple. "I play with my breasts for a long time. I like to build."

Ffffuck. He whipped the truck onto a side street. *Good enough.* Nobody would see them there. The first benefit of having your town wiped out by a tornado—sex in the open was easier.

She arched, bringing her breasts into sharp relief. He shoved the truck into park and reached for her. When her tight peaks were trapped under his fingers and her mouth was under his, he was in his private acre of heaven.

Why settle for an acre when I can have the whole ranch? He was free, she was free. There wasn't a brotherly thought in his whole skull.

She gathered her legs beneath her so she was kneeling on the seat, her arms around his neck and her tongue driving him mad. Feeling her hair slip against her bare skin sent him into paroxysms of need.

With a groan, he yanked her across the console into his lap. She squeaked as her ass thumped into his erection, and the damn little hellcat started to wiggle as if trying to screw his cock into her.

He pummeled her mouth with his kisses even as he pinched, twisted and stroked her nipples. She managed to work the buttons of his shirt. When her warm flesh met his, he couldn't take it another minute. He yanked open the door, gathered her against his chest and carried her to the back of the truck.

She was savvy enough to open the tailgate, and then he dragged her up the bed like a big cat hauling his prey into a tree. When she made a strangled noise, he broke the kiss.

"What is it?"

"The truck's freezing."

"Damn. I'll get a blanket." Every cowboy— and cowgirl—had a flashlight, matches, and a blanket in his truck, but why was his so far away? It took precious seconds to go to the cab and locate the soft fleece behind the seat. Longer to spread it beneath Danica, but she stretched out immediately.

"Glad to see you haven't cooled off too much." He latched onto her throat, sucking until she writhed. With one hand, he unfastened the shorts that had been driving him up a wall—even without a wall left in Los Vista.

"Not on your life. I've been waiting weeks for this." She tugged his shirt down his arms, and he maneuvered to let her strip it from him. Pressure mounted in his groin with every passing second. He ground his cock against her thigh even as he dipped his fingers into the opening he'd made in her shorts.

When he found her pussy dripping wet, he dropped his face to her breasts and prayed for strength. He didn't know how long he could hold back, but he was damn well going to make her scream twice before he took his ease in her tight body.

He gained his knees. "Put your arms over your head. That's a good girl. Don't move them."

Her eyes glittered as she obeyed. The glint of her belly ring made his cock stretch farther.

With quick, efficient movements, he stripped off her Daisy Dukes and her scrap of panties. The shadow between her legs made him feel like a kid on Christmas morning, opening his long-coveted package.

Seeing her bare at last, spread under the stars for him...it was too good to be true. He nudged her thighs apart. Then hiking his knee against her pussy, he leaned over her for a kiss. The minute her searing, damp heat engulfed his knee, he grunted. She issued a feminine moan that drove him crazier.

Dragging his mouth away, he grated out, "Rub yourself against my thigh. Let me see how you take care of yourself, darlin'."

A mewl left her as she arched into his leg. Even through the layer of denim, she was burning hot. Ripe and needy. He wished he were naked too, but having his cock anywhere near her would drive him off the cliff of control.

With a hand on her ass and one on her breast, he guided her slow, rolling movements against his thigh. The scents of arousal fogged his brains. In conjunction with the clean country air, he couldn't get enough. He filled his lungs as she ground her sweet pussy against him.

"That's it. Take what you need. I know you've been aching all day just like I have."

She made a noise of agreement, her nails blunt in his back. When he met her gaze, her lips popped open in an O and her panting breaths came faster.

"Come on, darlin'. Come for me."

His command sent her flying. As shudders racked her body, he held her gaze, refusing to let her look away.

A final groan left her, and he swallowed it with his kiss. Twining his tongue with hers and tasting her passion. When she bit into his lower lip, he reared back and did what he'd been throbbing to do for days—he whipped open his fly and shoved his jeans and boxers down his hips.

She reached for his cock.

"No, little wench. Not yet. You're at my mercy right now because as soon as you put your hands on me, I'm going to give up control. We do this on my terms. Okay?"

Her labored breathing made her breasts rise and fall. "Yes." Her voice was faint with desire.

"Keep your arms over your head or I'll tie them up."

"What if I disobey you?"

He gave her a wolfish grin as he tugged off his boots. "Then I'll spank you. Now keep your hands above your head."

Her eyelids shuddered as he took his cock in hand. "I want to taste you, Brodie."

Liquid heat threatened to erupt, but he bit back his need. "You want my cock in your throat?"

"God, yes."

His skin prickled as he knee-walked up the bed of the truck and angled his cock toward her pretty lips. She extended her tongue to reach him.

Fuck yeah. "Open your mouth, darlin'. Take me inside."

She didn't waste a heartbeat. As his cock was sucked into her hot depths, he threw his head back with a guttural moan. She drew on his length and did something with her tongue on the underside that almost sent him over the ledge. He didn't want to think about where she'd practiced such a trick, but he wasn't going to complain.

His balls tightened against his body. Rocking his hips, he sank into her throat. Heart drumming, he reveled in the feel of being inside her. It was only going to be better once he was buried in her sweet pussy.

She sucked his throbbing head like the greediest of women. Oh God, he couldn't last if she kept that up. He pulled free of her mouth. "Don't move."

She gave a quiet sound of disappointment but stared up at him and waited for her next instruction.

Hell, he could get used to this. He'd never been with a woman this way, and he had no idea where his dominating nature was coming from now. But he wasn't going to question it—she was giving him exactly what he needed.

"Brodie." His name came out as almost a plea.

He grabbed his jeans and removed the wallet from the pocket. Thank God he located the condom the first try because his hands were shaking with lust. If he didn't get inside her soon...

"Open your legs wide for me." His order was immediately obeyed as he slid the condom over his aching length in one smooth glide. When he lowered himself between her luscious thighs and looked into her gleaming eyes, he stopped thinking about the why-nots.

* * * * *

As Brodie sank into her pulsating folds, she cried out. Latched her legs around him and without asking his permission, put her arms around him too. He didn't protest—just started to move.

Each ridge of his steely cock against her inner walls was felt in every corner of her body. Wild to connect him to her further, she found his mouth and kissed him. Tongues swirled as he jerked his hips. Bringing his cock deep, deeper.

And when he eased a fingertip over her clit and ground it into her body, a wave of pleasure rushed her. A release struck, towed her into the hot depths of ecstasy. She barely dragged in a full breath before he was lifting her ass to meet his thrusts, his face fierce as he took what he needed from her at long last.

Watching his face contort sent her flying. "Brodie!" She clutched him to her as he claimed yet another orgasm from her. Contractions stole over her.

His roar filled the night. In the back of her mind, she wondered if they were really far enough away from the Kents and their friends. Then she stopped caring as Brodie turned his lips to hers and delivered such a tender kiss that tears jumped into her eyes.

She squeezed them shut against the happy sting and accepted everything this man could give her. What she could give him. He'd lost so much but she would do all in her power to restore him. If that meant he tied her up and had his way with her in every empty corner of Los Vista, she was on board. Small sacrifices and all that.

As her smile spread beneath his kiss, he made a huffing noise and drew away. She tightened her thighs around him, but he didn't attempt to leave her.

"What are you smiling about?" he rumbled.

"You. The stars. The way this blanket feels against my skin. I haven't had pleasure like this in so long, Brodie."

She felt him shift and stretch, as if preening at her words. Her smile grew. "I hope there're more condoms in your wallet because we don't have a convenience store anymore."

He snorted and held his rubber in place as he rolled off. She leaned onto one hip to gaze at his carved muscles in the moonlight. It wasn't her imagination that the lines of his shoulders were more relaxed. When he'd dealt with the condom and turned to her, she sucked in a sharp breath.

Concern lowered his eyebrows. "What is it? Cold again?"

"No," she choked out. "You're beautiful."

"Oh Danica." He curled into the blanket and drew her against him. With the heat of his body, she was far from cold, and it wouldn't be long before she was hot again. Rubbing herself off on his thigh had been a huge turn-on. She'd never had a man ask such a thing of her.

As he stroked her hair over and over, she clung to him. Pressing small kisses against his salty skin and learning his contours in the darkness.

Long minutes passed and neither spoke. Her mind worked fast and furious, though. Galloping ahead into a future. From the beginning, she'd known having Brodie in her life was right. Now that she could fully admit it to herself, she felt bad about giving Wayne another chance. She'd probably just confused him. The man wasn't what she was looking for. He didn't inspire her to go after a better life. Brodie did.

"Do you think the Kent children will ever go to sleep? They were so excited," she said.

His chest vibrated under her ear as he chuckled. "They were. I bet little Hallie gets out of her tent tonight and they find her on the swing in the morning."

She giggled at the mental image. "What we did today felt good."

His arms flexed around her, bringing her closer. "Everything about today has felt good, darlin'."

His words burrowed deep into her soul and joy spread through her. "So how do we hold onto that feeling?"

Skimming a kiss over her brow, he said, "We have that town meeting you mentioned."

"Hmm."

"You sound disappointed. Did you have another plan in mind?"

"Yes, I do." Walking her fingers around his hip, she stroked her thumb down his cock, slowly to the tip. His shaft stirred and it began to elongate.

* * * * *

She was going to kill him. He'd survived bombs and bullets only to come home and suffer a slow, erotic death.

He caught her wrist as she began to stroke him. "Hold up. You're not in charge here, darlin'."

As a soft coo bubbled past her lips, a wild need to tame and claim her settled over him. He reached for his abandoned shirt.

"What are you doing?"

He caught her wrists and began to twine the long sleeves of his Western shirt around them. She quivered when he tugged the knot tight. "Can you feel your hands?"

"Yes." She wiggled, proving she had enough room but couldn't escape.

A crooked smile stretched his mouth. "Perfect." He raked his gaze over her. She was better than perfect. God, when had she grown up? He didn't care—he was going to take full advantage of that *and* the second condom he'd stuffed in his wallet.

When he rolled her onto her hands and knees, splaying a hand on her lower back, she twisted to see him. "Brodie, what—"

"Shh." He caressed her rounded ass cheek. Then the other. The flesh bounced deliciously, and his cock bobbed against his abs. "I know you're wet for me, darlin'. Spread your legs apart a little and let me see."

She did better than that. She rested on her elbows and arched her back, sending her tight ass into the air.

"Fuck yeahhhh." He gazed hotly at the crease of her ass and the tight little pucker beckoning to him. And farther down, her wet pussy folds. "Hold that pose."

Without warning, he dipped his head and kissed the seam of her ass. She gasped. When he pressed tiny kisses upward then snaked his tongue around her pucker, she gulped back a cry.

Damn, she was so receptive. Fireworks of excitement burst behind his eyes as he lapped a circle around her ridged entrance then moved swiftly lower to plunge his tongue into her core. Her walls clenched around his tongue. They both groaned. Juices coated his mouth.

Reaching beneath her, he located her hard nubbin and trapped it with his thumb. Harsh noises left her, and she pushed against his hand and mouth.

"Fucking sexy little wench. Are you going to come so soon?" He sucked her wetly until she couldn't hold still. The movements of her body were voice enough. Gently he stroked her clit while drawing on her pussy with his lips and tongue.

She trembled more and more. He backed off, and she pushed out a ragged breath. "Noooo."

"I'm not ready to let you come yet, darlin'. You're a greedy girl and you've already had what? Three orgasms?"

A muffled noise of discontent came from her, which only fueled his need. What was it about handling her this way? Taking charge of her body and pleasure was giving him much more than a swollen cock.

He scraped his teeth lightly over the curve of her ass, and she jerked backward for more. But he lifted his head and wound an arm around her middle. As he flipped her onto her back, he caught her gaze. Her eyes were fever-bright and her lips swollen as if she'd been biting them.

Rubbing the thumb he'd circled her clit with over her lower lip, he said, "Taste yourself."

Her tongue darted out to skim his thumb.

Barely harnessing his growl, he dipped his thumb into her mouth and let her taste. Then he pulled his wet thumb free and painted her nipple until it stood erect in the cooler night air.

"Brodie, please. I need to touch you."

"Not yet." God, he loved hearing her beg. He wanted her screaming for mercy as he gave her a tenth orgasm. He trailed his fingers up her inner thighs. She parted for him, but not wide enough. He needed her splayed to him.

"Put your foot up here." He patted the side of the truck. Her face registered surprise, but she was willing. Fuck, this was going to kill him when he left her at home tonight.

When she settled her heel on the side, he strummed her wet folds. Her pussy grew wetter. He needed her spread wider. "And up here. Can you stretch?"

Her truck wasn't one of the massive ones often seen on ranches, but the bed was wide enough that it was good she had long legs. Her toes pointed as she struggled to give him what he wanted.

Which was a view of her scorched into his brain. A photograph he could take away and pull out again and again. Holding her gaze, he rumbled, "Good girl," and plunged two fingers into her hot, wet sheath.

* * * * *

Danica was melting beneath his electrical gaze and the ferocious desire inside her. Having Brodie at all was amazing, but finding he was kinky surprised the hell out of her. Her experiences seemed lame in comparison to this night with Brodie. Maybe she'd always known she needed something more with men.

He locked his gaze on her face as he finger-fucked her with deep, fast strokes. Each pass of his fingertips over her G-spot made her flood with juices. In seconds he had her hanging from the edge of a monumental drop.

She tightened, quivering.

When he pulled his fingers free, she cried out with displeasure—and gained a light spank on her pussy for her insolence.

She cried out as white-hot desire pushed her higher.

"You like that, little wench?" With his palm over her pussy, she craved the heat as well as the pleasure-pain.

"Uhhhh." Forgetting her hands were bound, she reached for him.

He slapped her once more with just enough sting to steal her breath. Her pussy flooded.

And he began to finger her again. Slowly this time, using his entire body it seemed. His shoulder muscles flexed and he grunted as if it pained him to fill her with only his fingers. She begged with her eyes until she saw some cord in him snap.

"Come for me, darlin'. Come on my fingers." He added a third and wedged it high in her pussy. Being stretched sent her overboard. As waves of ecstasy pulsed around her, she clung to the life raft that was Brodie.

Still gasping, she didn't realize he'd removed his fingers until the fat head of his cock smoothed over her folds. He hovered over her and claimed her mouth at the same time he took her body.

"Keep your legs spread. Open yourself to me." His gritty words were flames in her soul. She'd do anything to please him.

Spreading her thighs, she jerked against each thrust. Taking him to the hilt, her inner walls closing around his every withdrawing

236

movement. When his eyes grew as dark as sin, she surged upward for his kiss.

"Can I put my arms around your neck?" Her breathless question must have pleased him, because he stiffened. His body gleamed blue in the moonlight, and cords stood out in his throat with the effort to hold back, it seemed.

"Yes," he said roughly.

The minute her bound wrists were looped around his neck, he caught her hip in one hand, hitched her leg over his shoulder, and began to slowly send her off the deep end. He moved like an erotic dancer, rolling his hips. Then he kissed her, and she couldn't hold back another second.

She yanked him close, his name leaving her as he pounded her into a mindlessness she never wanted to recover from. As his body quaked and a roar passed his lips, she floated down, down, knowing this was far more than a simple fuck in the bed of a truck.

This was life-altering. Soul-binding. This was her future.

Chapter Eight

The scuff of a boot on the worn barn floor shouldn't affect Danica so much. But knowing the man who'd made that sound was near sent her into a whirlwind of emotion.

She poked her head out of the stall to see him walking down the center aisle. Too easily she could see him in combat—face fierce, eyes alert. He looked as though he was on a mission.

Maybe that mission's me.

They'd parted in the wee hours. Nothing had been said about their time together. Speaking would ruin the moment. Besides, there was plenty of time to discuss their encounter.

He spotted her. When she realized he wasn't smiling, she carefully set her shovel against the wooden wall and stepped out.

"Hey, cowboy." She tried for lighthearted, but he looked anything but. *Shit.*

"We need to talk about last night."

No dancing around the subject. And definitely no grabbing her and shoving her against a barn wall while he kissed her boneless.

She dragged in a breath of barn air. Some stale, some not. But the scents of home fortified her, which was good because she had a feeling she was about to do battle with this sergeant.

He stopped before her. "I need to know if you're okay."

That surprised her enough to scramble her thoughts. "Why wouldn't I be okay?"

"What happened...between us..." He pushed out a noisy breath. Agitation was written across the lines of his shoulders, but she wasn't about to help him along. He was a grown man—let him speak his mind.

"Last night," he went on.

"What about last night?"

"Dammit, Danica, don't play that with me."

She arched a brow. "I'm just seeing where your head's at, Brodie."

"What's that supposed to mean?"

"You go all Rambo on me, stomping up the center of the barn and saying we need to talk about last night. Am I supposed to believe you're coming to give me a repeat performance?"

Something shivered over his features. For two heartbeats, the flow of his expression was disrupted. Then abruptly it settled into a mask. "What we shared was—"

In one long step she came up against him. "Passionate, sexy…fun as hell?"

His throat worked. "Danica."

She skimmed his shirt buttons with one fingertip. "Don't ruin last night by overthinking it, Brodie. It was just sex."

"What?" he barked, face reddening. "Just sex?"

"Well yeah. Isn't that what you were about to say? Lust, physical release and all that horse crap?"

He stared at her. Beneath his gaze her nipples hardened and a heat began to build, low. "Son of a bitch," he said so softly she might have missed it if she hadn't seen his mouth move.

She took a step backward. He stalked forward. Her inner playfulness popped up, ready for a game of chase. And this was definitely the man to play with. Taking another step backward, she said, "Please go on, Brodie. Tell me what's on your mind."

A big arm snaked out and snagged her around the middle. She squealed as he ripped her off her feet and planted her before him.

Not a sliver of hay could fit between their bodies, which meant she could feel every solid muscle in him

And especially one in his jeans. She tipped her face up to meet his gaze.

"It was not just sex, Danica, and you know it."

"'Course I do, cowboy. So you're admitting it?"

"You always did talk too damn much." His eyes were hooded as he swooped in and claimed her lips.

* * * * *

Brodie walked through the glass doors into the cool interior of the bank. Since this branch was in the adjoining town, he'd never been inside, but the cool air made him breathe a sigh of relief. His father's truck didn't have air conditioning, which meant his shirt clung to his spine and his hair was damp beneath his hat. But he couldn't complain when he was borrowing the truck. It was a little depressing to think in about four minutes his bank account would be wiped out, with no hope of buying a vehicle of his own.

He sidled up to the teller and recognition flared in her eyes. He stared at her for a second, riffling through the files of his mind until one popped out.

Pointing at her, he said, "You were friends with Danica Pope in high school." Visions of oversized glasses and a messy ponytail flashed through his mind.

"That's right." She nodded enthusiastically. Her ponytail had been replaced by a sleek bob that graced her jaw, and the glasses were a thing of the past.

He read her name on the gold plate. "Nice to see you again, Kendall."

"Welcome home, soldier."

"Thank you. Are you living in town here?"

She smiled but there was a sadness in her eyes. "Not many places to live or work in Los Vista."

Pressing his lips together, he nodded. "That's true."

"I heard you're working the ranches — yours and the Popes'."

"Yep. We're hoping to do some building, get some houses for people who never left. And hopefully we'll bring people back."

"Really? That would be great." Her white smile went on for miles.

"So you think Los Vista residents would want to come home?"

"I do. A lot of them dream of it, but it's easier, faster, and sometimes cheaper to buy an existing home than to build."

"That's a problem for sure. But we can't let our town disappear, can we?"

"I hope it doesn't, though I don't have much to contribute, I'm afraid. I need to work and living close to the bank makes sense."

A weight slipped into his stomach. He'd realized restoring their town wouldn't be easy, but her words were discouraging. Hundreds of people must feel the same way she did. And how many with families had just taken their insurance money straight to the next town and paid for a home?

There had to be a way. He wasn't going to watch Los Vista fill up with tumbleweeds.

He made his transaction and a cashier's check was cut. With it in hand, he went outside into the oppressive humidity again. When he got to his pa's truck, he spotted one of the old-timers who was good friends with his father leaning against the side.

"Aha!" he said as Brodie approached. "I knew this truck belonged to a Bell!" He came forward to pump Brodie's hand and slap his shoulder. "Welcome home, young man. Glad to see you whole."

We don't all have the luxury of being whole.

"I appreciate it, Mr. Callahan. So you're living here now?"

"Yeah, I miss the old place, but ranchin' was getting beyond me. With no children willing to take over, it was time to hang up my reins. But I sure miss the land. Sure do." He looked off into the distant park with manicured shrubs and a monument to past war heroes.

"So you wouldn't consider coming back even if you had a new house on your land?"

"Considered it. But in the end, I was ready for a change of scenery and Margaret was interested in one of those condominiums with a pool. In this weather, that water is welcome." He leaned near and spoke from the corner of his lips. "Besides, there's a lot of honeys who live around us. The view might not be fields and cattle but it's nothing to turn your head from!"

Brodie chuckled at the old man's joke though that weighty feeling was back and it had brought ten friends. He listened to Mr. Callahan talk for several more minutes before parting with the excuse he had work to do on the ranch.

He wasn't lying—he and Danica were finishing the enclosure. And one of his goals would be realized later that day with a shipment that would surprise Danica. Things were taking shape on the ranch.

But really it pained Brodie to talk to people of Los Vista who weren't willing to make their lives there again. Maybe he was naïve for believing the town was savable.

Suddenly he wanted to talk it out with Danica. To tuck her against his chin and tell her his worries.

He snorted as he got behind the wheel and started the engine. When he looked up, he knew he'd done it again—lost track of time. He'd been staring for long minutes while his mind roamed over so many troubles—his and Danica's, all of their parents', his friends', and so much more.

When he rumbled up the drive to the Popes' place, Danica was on the porch with a dark figure at her feet. Crow. The dog gathered himself and walked to the steps. Happy to see the old hound, Brodie found himself smiling when he got out of the truck.

Danica drifted to the steps too.

Brodie looked up at her, chest tight with emotion. *You look like an angel this morning.*

He couldn't say that—he needed to keep his distance for her sake. Sooner or later they'd need to talk about their slip-ups. Their crazy-hot, passion-filled nights he couldn't erase from his memory.

She cocked a brow and a hip, thrusting it forward and tapping a foot. "You're late. Don't think I don't know you were avoiding cleaning stalls with me today." She scolded him about the stalls but her tone held a note of worry.

"Damn, I did miss it. I'm sorry. I had to run into the next town." She stood so close, wearing yet another pair of Daisy Dukes. It seemed she'd cut off every pair of jeans in her closet. He was wrapped in her spell once again.

I'll stop lusting after her this afternoon.

He wrapped his fingers around her warm thigh. Electricity zapped between them, but it didn't stop her sass.

"Well, you're not too tired to finish the enclosure?"

"No."

"Where were you?" she pressed.

"Had something to do in town."

Her expression grew solemn. "Oh."

Her cool word held a world of meaning. She drew from his touch and put distance between them. Immediately he wanted her back. He ached to press her against the wall of the house and give her what she wanted—what they both needed.

Mounting the first step, he held her gaze.

"I know you're brushing me off, Brodie. It's not going to work."

When faced with her direct stare and bold words, he took the coward's way. Scuffing his boot on the step, he said, "I'm not trying to do or not do anything. I thought you were helping your ma in the garden this morning."

Danica's lovely face shivered with an emotion he couldn't name. Until she said, "She won't get out of bed. I've done the weeding."

They exchanged a somber look. Danica's eyes were dark with pain.

"C'mere." Brodie tugged her off the top step into his arms. She came easily, warm and pliant against his chest. When her hair caught on the scruff on his jaw, his heart did a flipping thing. More and more that was happening, but he was trying not to think about what his feelings for Danica were.

She was everything he needed right now—she was happiness, light, and comfort. Besides being a smart and capable rancher with sex appeal for miles.

Before he could act on the urge to pin her to the porch support and sink into her tight body, he let her go.

"So, Man of Five Words, do I get to know what you were doing in town?" She directed a tendril of hair behind her ear.

"You'll see soon enough." He checked his watch. "You finish all the chores this morning?"

"Yeah, no thanks to you. I thought we were a team, Brodie." Her teasing tone held an undercurrent, and he looked closely at her face.

"Just how upset are you with me?"

"Depends on how willing you are to make up." She leaned in, her full lips as inviting as sin.

He was having a hard time keeping his hands off her and she knew it. From deep inside he dragged up a grain of self-control—just one. A little one. But it was enough.

"Let's get to work on that fence."

She shot him the same crestfallen look she'd given Matt and the guys when they told her she couldn't tag along.

To soften his words, he reached for her hand. She took it, and they crossed the yard to the barn. There they saddled their horses in silence and then rode out. Her quiet mare still didn't like the horse of his choosing, but she was becoming more tolerant. When Brodie rode beside her, the animal kept her ears on alert but didn't dance away.

"I ran into your friend Kendall in town."

Danica swung her head his direction, and once more the breath was punched from him. He'd never get used to seeing her in full cowgirl glory, shoulders straight and hair streaming.

"Oh?"

"Yes, I asked if she'd come back to Los Vista and she said it would be nice but her job keeps her there."

"That's too bad, but it's only one person from Los Vista, Brodie." It was so like her to read between the lines and realize he was worrying about more townspeople refusing to come home.

"Actually it was two. I ran into Callahan too."

As they rode, they discussed some of the old-timers not wanting to start over again. It was understandable—they were settled. But that meant the foundation of Los Vista was crumbling. Without the people who'd held it together, would they ever be able to build or was the ground too shaky?

"I think we'd best hold that town meeting," Brodie said.

"Soon."

They reached the enclosure. A few bits of fencing and a gate had been deposited in the grass, waiting for them to finish. Today was the day. Fully merging the two ranches wouldn't bring back the whole town but it was a start.

Danica swung from her saddle with so much grace that his heart surged. When she bent to lift one of the fence posts, he bit off a growl at the sight of her fine curvy ass. Hearing it, she twisted and shot him a come-hither look, her behind still pointed his direction.

"Jesus, woman. You trying to kill me?" He rubbed a hand over his face even as he drifted toward her like a parched horse to water.

"Am I succeeding?" She wiggled her hips.

He was on her in a blink. Cupping her ass, he jerked his distended cock against the roundness. "Insatiable wench. I fucked you last night."

"And for three nights prior to that. Doesn't mean I've gotten enough."

Okay, so his self-control was dust. He was doing a piss-poor job of keeping his hands off her.

Reaching around her, he trapped one nipple between his fingers. He pinched hard enough that she whimpered but simultaneously shimmied her hips back into his cock.

"God, if I wasn't on a tight schedule, I'd make you scream four times."

"Only four? And what's the hurry?" She gave a slow, lazy roll of her hips that made his eyelids flutter.

"It's a surprise. Now get to work." He swatted her behind. The crack made her horse shy away and Danica cry out.

Before he went back on his decision to leave her alone for the time being, he grabbed a shovel that had been leaning against the finished fence. The scent of loamy earth filled his nostrils. The rhythm of hard work soothed him, though his libido still raged.

After they'd erected two posts and filled the gaps with barbed wire, they were ready for the gate. The sun was climbing high, and sweat beaded on his neck as he worked. Danica wiped her forehead several times and took a break to drink some water.

"I can't believe we're nearly finished. Think of the free time we'll have when we're not fixing or building fence." Her insinuating tone was a dark whip to his senses.

He gave her a crooked smile. "Yeah, because ranching only takes a few hours a day."

She laughed at his joke. "You know what I mean. Joining our fences means the herd will have more room to roam. We won't be moving them around as much to find better grazing land."

"That's true. But we'll have new goals. Like putting in that late corn crop. Making hay."

"Rolling in it." She twitched her hips his direction, and he issued a groan.

Dragging his focus away from her sexy body was a hard test, but he managed.

"You keep checking your watch. What's going on, Pup?"

He rolled his eyes at her nickname. "Got something to do in about half an hour. We gotta rush this. Here, grab the other side."

The gate was a final addition to the enclosure. It would be kept open to combine the ranches. But if they ever wanted, they could return to their original separation. The idea of not being part of her everyday life stabbed him.

He glanced at her beautiful face and prayed nothing would ever happen to make him fall out of her good graces. Sleeping with her was a risk, and eventually he'd need to put a stop to it. *Today. You promised it would be this afternoon.*

She won't remain single forever, a voice in the back of his mind said. He cringed from thoughts of her marrying, of having little cowboys and cowgirls who would run this land just as they had. His chest tightened.

Dammit.

When the gate was installed, they stood back to look at their handiwork. At the same moment, they turned to each other. Danica threw herself at him. He caught her, hitching her legs around his waist as he claimed her mouth.

Sweet flavors burst in his mouth while passion flowed like honey through his veins.

259

She parted her lips for him, and he plunged his tongue inside. She moaned, angling to give him deeper access even as her hands roved over his shoulders and back.

He kissed her until his lips tingled and he was as hard as steel. Still, it wasn't enough. He feared it never would be.

When she tore from the kiss, her eyes were fever-bright. "Surely we have a few minutes."

He pinched her backside, which was a mistake because she pushed her damp, hot pussy against him. Fuck, what risks he'd take to stroke her to orgasm. To watch her come apart and feel her juices spill over his fingers.

He'd face a firing squad to have it.

With a smooth motion, he let her drop to the ground. Clasping her face in his hands, he walked her backward until the gate was at her spine. Then he held her gaze while one-handedly unbuttoning her shorts.

"You're making me burn up, Brodie. Hurry." Her panting breaths threatened to knock him to his knees, but he remained upright. His fingers met hot, silky flesh. He eased his hand into her panties, stretching the cotton. Holding her gaze, he probed the top of her seam.

Her clit was a ripe berry beneath his finger. And she was wild in seconds. Rocking against his hand, slick with need. He captured her mouth once more as he circled her clit. She leaned on the fence heavily, legs splayed, small cries escaping her.

He sank a finger into her, and wild need tore through him. He dragged her closer, straining with the urge to join them with his cock. When he alternated between fingering her deep and toying with her nubbin, he felt her tense.

"God, Brodie. I'm so close."

"Come on my fingers, darlin'. Say my name."

Because that's not possessive as hell.

He didn't care about anything right now except feeling her come apart for him.

Squeaking gasps left her. Her pussy was so damn slippery, and he was about to skid out of control, drop his Wranglers, and fuck her here and now.

"Brod—" Her choked cry cut off halfway; her legs quivered. He crushed her lips beneath his as she tipped over the edge and came. For a mindless minute, he floated with her in an erotic haze, stretching her release with slower swirls of his fingertip.

A final shudder racked her, and she collapsed against him, twisting the fabric of his shirt.

"Fuck, you're beautiful when you come." He stared at her through lowered lids. Her cheeks were pink, her lips plump. And her eyes... Damn, he didn't deserve a woman who looked at him like that.

He slid his finger back and forth over her nubbin a few more times. She jerked in his hold, and his cock was impossibly hard. But he couldn't sink into her slippery heat right now.

Withdrawing his hand, he fastened her fly again. Then he couldn't stop himself from sticking his fingers into his mouth and sucking. Her cheeks grew pinker, and a rumble left him, half need, half regret. He wanted her with a fury, but once they started several hours would be lost to total bliss.

"We've gotta go."

"Where?" she asked, still leaning on the gate, her palms on his chest for support.

"Back to the ranch. We've got someone to meet."

* * * * *

Danica blinked at the cattle being driven off the truck and into her pasture. Young ones for the most part. And a few mature animals that could be used for reproduction. All in all, a hell of a lot of money had been laid down for this new herd.

Brodie's face was alive with excitement. "What do you think, darlin'?"

Her heart expanded to see him happy — but deep down she felt betrayed. Wasn't this their combined operation? Their fathers had given them free rein of their ranches, but Brodie wasn't including her in decisions?

Swallowing hard, she said, "It's unexpected. How did you do it?"

"When you're at war, you don't have a lot of places to spend money. I had a little egg sitting there and I decided it would be better used here." He stretched a hand toward the milling beasts.

Suddenly Danica felt small and mean for being upset that Brodie hadn't shared this decision with her. He'd put his life on the line for that money, and whatever he did with it was totally within his right.

"It's a new crossbreed," he was saying. "They mature faster, which means—"

"We can sell them faster."

"Right." His eyes gleamed.

She caught a little of his joy and looked at the herd with fresh eyes. She saw the potential roaming around her pasture, not only some betrayal of their agreement. He'd done this for the good of all of them.

Catching his hand, she squeezed his fingers. "This is great, Brodie."

He brought her knuckles to his lips and skimmed them with a kiss that made her throat tighten. He hadn't been home for very long, and he'd seen her as a woman instead of a child for a lot less time. But she'd never felt this way about any man. If she was honest, she could see him as a permanent fixture in her life.

But she still felt his reluctance. Even while he peeled her off the stars, she felt him holding back.

When he handed the fat cashier's check to the man delivering the cattle, Brodie was nothing but smiles. Her heart flipped at the sheer male beauty before her. She wanted to see more happiness shining in his eyes.

He drifted to stand close to her. Shoulder to shoulder they watched the driver head back to the main road.

"My first real purchase. Look at them." He propped his hands on the fence and stared at the animals.

"A lot of branding to do."

"There's that. I'll ask Wydell to help."

"He'll like that. He seems to prefer ranching to demolition."

"That's backbreaking work. And in this case soul-breaking. He's ripping apart people's lives."

Deep in thought, she tugged on her earlobe and her earring back fell off. The silver stud fell and struck Brodie's boot. With lightning swiftness, he dropped into a crouch. His nimble fingers closed around the bright object, and then he popped to his feet.

The movement left her breathless. His muscles bulged with the predatory action, and she was left to think about his years spent as a soldier instead of a rancher.

All day long she couldn't shake the feeling that he was two different men trying to merge into one. As they checked over the cattle's health, she envisioned him leading men into combat. When his big hands moved to do a task, she only saw him running the chamber of a weapon.

What was it about today that had her looking at him differently? Maybe her heart was trying to take in the whole Brodie.

As he strode in her direction, his arms swinging at his sides and his hat tipped low, her nipples hardened. Low in her belly, the familiar ache began.

He glanced at her as he went into the barn. *Coming, cowboy. I'll follow you into a cave full of rattlesnakes.*

Before he could grab some horse tack, she landed a hand on his chest, over his pounding heart. "A good day's work, lover."

"Danica…"

"Why do you try to stop yourself, Brodie? You know you want to give in." She swayed against him.

He clasped her hip. "We shouldn't be doing this."

"Why?" She wasn't acting coy—she genuinely had no clue why they should try to stay away from each other. They were both free, and they were like biscuits and gravy. Everything about them worked. Why was he denying it?

"Because of Matt." His roughly spoken words fell between them.

Understanding dawned over her. Feeling an icy grip, she took a step back. "You think Matt would disapprove of what's between us?"

He stared into her eyes for two long heartbeats. Then he twisted away. "I don't know."

She cupped his jaw and turned his head back to study his face. "You do. Why would you think that?"

"Maybe because—" He broke off, throat working and eyes downcast.

"Wait. Don't tell me he told you on his deathbed to stay away from his sister."

Brodie's gaze flashed to hers, angry and intense. "Don't talk about that."

"I know it hurts you. It guts me to think about it and I wasn't even there."

"Stop."

"He wouldn't be upset with his best friend for making his sister happy."

He went still. "Is that what I do, Danica?" His burning whisper scorched her senses.

A loaded silence hung between them. One shift and the balance would be disrupted — he could end things and she could go off in tears. But she wasn't going to back down. He was worth fighting for, even if it was his personal demon she was trying to slay.

She nodded. "My parents are living in the dark of their grief. All my friends are gone and I only have an occasional paper to look forward to writing for my college course. That and a butt-load of work on a ranch that is depressing and lonely as hell. What do you think, Brodie?"

His chest gave a violent shudder as if he were harnessing something wild. The crease of his jaw fluttered beneath her fingers.

With his basic-training swiftness, he plucked her off her feet. His lips crashed over hers as he spun her to a wall, her legs hoisted around him. An uneven moan ripped from her chest, and he answered with a sound like a wild beast.

Their mouths collided. She surrendered to the bruising violence in his kiss. Wanting everything about this beautiful, hardworking, life-weary man. She pushed off his hat and threaded her fingers in the strands of his hair.

He thrust his cock toward her pussy. "You and your damn cutoffs. I can't stay away from you," he gasped between carnal kisses.

"I've got three pairs you haven't even seen yet."

His growl vibrated from the ends of her hair to her toes. When he slowly levered away and started stripping off her top, her heart constricted at the sight of his fierce expression.

God, he was a beautiful man, and she was in love with him. It had happened weeks ago, in the moment he'd brought Matt home to her and cried with her on the front porch. She'd given her heart to Brodie. Her childhood friend, her lover. He'd always been family, and now she wanted him in a whole new way.

Brodie was losing his damn mind to this woman. As he clamped his lips around her nipple and drew it into a tight peak, he tried to care about his vow to stay away from her. But her admission that he made her happy—well that was a personal crack he hadn't realized he was addicted to until this minute.

He sucked on her breast, tugging long moans from her. When she skidded a hand down his chest to his waist, he couldn't hold back another second. He needed to be inside her—now.

Letting her slide to her feet, he one-handedly worked open his belt and jeans while she dropped those tormenting shorts over her lush curves. His cock popped into his hand, and he stroked it. Once, twice.

The flash in her eyes was his only warning before she dropped to her knees and took his hard cock in her scorching hot mouth. With a growl, he fisted her hair, gazing at her closed eyes and sweet lips working him.

"Take it, darlin'. All of it." His command unleashed something primal inside him, and he churned his hips, feeding her every inch. She mewled around him, which only fueled him more.

Need mounted way too fast. As she ran her tongue around his head, he bit off a groan. Dragging her up his body, he speared her with two fingers. She cried out as he filled her body.

"Come for me. Come on my fingers then I'll pin you to this wall and fuck you until you don't know your name." He latched onto her throat, sucking and kissing while he fingered her hard and fast. When the heel of his hand bumped her clit repeatedly, he felt her tense.

With a wicked grin, he ground his palm against her nub.

"Please, Brodie."

"You need to come, darlin'. Trust me to take you there. Let go, my beautiful angel." He dragged his lips and tongue up her neck to the corner of her lips. As her orgasm hit, she turned her mouth against his.

Body racking with shudders of release, she couldn't support her weight. He held her as she flew. Only after juices had flooded his fingers and her gasps slowed did he locate one of several condoms he'd been carrying daily and slid it on.

Her eyes were bright with ecstasy and a light that made him feel like a better man. With her, he no longer dwelled on his number of kills or friends he'd lost. He just lived.

In one smooth glide, he filled her. She wrapped her leg around his hip and towed him closer even as he kept his promise to pin her to the wall. He trapped her hands overhead, their fingers meshed. Her sweet breath rushed over his lips as he pushed in all the way.

"So fucking tight. Squeeze me, darlin'."

Her inner walls flexed, and he issued a harsh noise. She closed the gap and kissed him, her mouth wild and her body wilder. She bucked against him, bringing him so…damn…deep.

Passion flowed. He stopped thinking about the broken town and her broken parents. About how his friends were so stressed they weren't their normal joking selves. With each push into Danica's tight body, he found the happiness she claimed he gave her.

Reaching between them, he pressed her clit. Her pussy clenched around him. "Fuck, you're soaking wet for me."

"All for you," she rasped.

That was all it took. His orgasm tore up from his balls and he jerked his hips with each jet of come. She stiffened. Cried out. He held her through the deluge of sensations inside him. Only when he broke the kiss and nuzzled her did he realize what she was giving him.

Something new to hope for.

* * * * *

Wydell plopped a frosty six-pack onto the center of the table they had set up in Brodie's barn for poker. "I brought the beer. Hope someone else brought the honeys."

Brodie gave him a crooked grin as his other two buddies dropped into their seats. "Lots of honeys in here." He twitched his chin toward the stalls on the right. "Over there you've got a couple good palominos. And that stall to the left is a horse about to foal."

"Asshole. At least tell me you brought the peanuts."

Reaching to the floor beside him, Brodie grabbed a metal pail filled with peanuts. As soon as they all set eyes on the contents, silence descended. The last time they'd all gathered around a poker table, Matt had come bearing a big bag of peanuts he'd bribed someone in one of the cook tents to get.

What'd you offer for them – your sister? Wydell had teased.

Scuffing a hand over his jaw, Brodie tried to dispel the ghost of a man who'd taken offense to the remark. *Let's get something straight. You don't even talk about my baby sister unless you gargle with mouthwash first. She's too good for you dickheads.*

Grabbing a peanut, Brodie cracked it in two and dumped the little rounds into his palm. He tossed them into his mouth and chewed as he reached for a beer. The other guys dug into the drinks and snacks.

Nobody spoke for a minute, and then Boyd said, "So Garrett, how's your mom?"

Laughter erupted, breaking the tension, as Garrett turned his black gaze on them. "Lay off my mother."

"What was she wearing when you left?" Boyd pushed.

"You son of a bitch." Garrett launched to his feet and Boyd took off. Wydell and Brodie watched them lap the barn, laughing.

"Oh God, my sides ache. I haven't laughed in forever," Brodie said, hunching around the cramping in his gut.

Boyd grabbed a pitchfork and wielded it at Garrett like a man holding off a werewolf. Garrett did look a little demented. His hat had fallen off somewhere, and his hair was a disheveled mop. All of them had gotten a little too long around the ears since taking their walking papers.

Brodie wiped a tear of mirth from the corner of his eye and picked up the cards. When he started to shuffle, the chase was forgotten, and the guys returned to their seats.

When Boyd sat on the overturned barrel, he took a whole handful of nuts and started cracking them rapid-fire.

"Slow down. The bucket's not going anywhere," Brodie said.

"Gotta keep up my energy in case Garrett gets sensitive about his mom again." He flashed a grin. "Besides, I worked my ass off all day pulling down beams of the Gatesman house."

As Brodie tapped the card deck into order, he scanned his buddies. While they were all just as big and badass as they always had been, he saw the strain the past weeks had put on their faces. Hollows beneath eyes, lines around mouths. Maybe they weren't eating or sleeping well either.

The first card hit the table.

"Where's Danica?" Wydell drawled.

Brodie stilled and looked at his friend. "Up at her house, I guess."

"You guess? I thought you'd know since you're banging her."

He almost choked on a nut. He sputtered and said, "What would give you that idea?"

"Couldn't be the way you can't keep your eyes off her." Garrett looked up with a crooked smile.

"Maybe we'd better shift our fantasies from Garrett's mom to Danica, boys." The joking light in Boyd's eyes was doused when he got a look at Brodie. He had no idea what his expression must look like, but if the building fury in his chest was any indication, Boyd had a good reason to cringe.

"I told you before to have some respect for Matt's sister."

"Sir, yes sir!" Wydell gave him a sharp salute, and after that things calmed down. The guys ate and drank. Another six-pack was produced and a hand was played. But Brodie couldn't shake the idea that he was so transparent when it came to Danica. He'd been trained to mask his emotions and never, ever give away the position of someone by staring at them.

Apparently when it came to Danica, his training flew out the window like a chicken chased by a fox. He cracked another beer and swigged, thinking of his last brush with alcohol. He wasn't about to make a similar mistake.

Talk turned to work around the town. Boyd related a story about finding a locked box in the debris of one house they'd demo'd last week. How he'd worked for twenty minutes to bust the lock, thinking he'd find birth certificates and savings bonds inside.

"What was it?" Garrett asked.

"Handcuffs."

They blinked at him. "You mean the homeowner was a cop?" Brodie asked.

"No," he said slowly. "I mean the people were into some kinky shit. Handcuffs, crops, a pair of nipple clamps."

"Well what'd you'd do with all of it?" Garrett asked.

"Put it away in a safe place."

"For what? You planning to go Dom/sub on us?"

Boyd shook off his friend's joke. "Not on your ass, no. You're not my type."

Garrett blew him a kiss, and Brodie sniggered. This was what he needed tonight. With their lives so far from what they'd imagined, they needed a ray of light.

"So what *are* you going to do with what was in the box, Boyd? Use it on Garrett's mom?" Wydell drawled.

"Oh you're asking for it." Garrett dropped his cards and lunged for Wydell. They hit the floor and rolled in a half-hearted wrestling match while Brodie and Boyd laughed at them.

"Good thing we're not playing for money," Boyd said with a shake of his head.

"None of us have any."

"True. Enough to live on for a little while until something big changes in this town."

They all exchanged glances. Each of them knew unless the tornado came through and put everything it had destroyed back in order, that wasn't likely to happen. But Brodie wasn't willing to discuss the matter right now — or even think about it. He just wanted to kick back with his friends and have a beer and some poker.

Once the guys were seated again and they'd played another hand — Brodie folded first — Boyd opened the topic of the mysterious box of sex toys again. "Any of you ever dominated a woman?"

Brodie kept his face perfectly even. He hadn't had time to consider why he needed to control Danica in the bedroom — and in the barn, in the field, and against the tractor tire. But it definitely fulfilled something inside him.

"Only once," Garrett said with a far-off expression.

They all looked to him.

"Pretty little thing the summer before we left for boot. She asked for it."

"Wait—what? Asked for it?" Boyd slid to the front of the barrel he was sitting on.

"Yeah, she asked me to tie her up and spank her."

"Whooeee."

"Jesus. Did you?" Wydell asked.

"What do you think, Hard-Ass?"

"I think your pecker curled up and hid, that's what."

Garrett was only half-joking when he growled, "Them's fighting words."

"So did ya tie her up and spank her?" Boyd asked.

"Fuck yeah. It was hot as hell." A private smile broke over Garrett's face. "A good memory to take to boot with me."

"Especially since you haven't had any action since." Wydell ducked Garrett's swing.

"You're one to talk. Been in love with your hand since seventh grade."

They all chuckled at that and settled back into the game.

"Speaking of secrets…" They all looked up at Garrett.

Brodie arched a brow. "What are you talking about?"

"Rumor has it a cattle truck drove into town and unloaded on the Pope Ranch."

Brodie pushed a breath through his nostrils. "There're rumors? There's only a dozen people in town. How are rumors being spread?"

"Twenty-eight people in town including us. And it's easy enough to hear talk when a lot of the residents come to chat while we work," Garrett said.

"So is it true?" Wydell drawled.

Brodie nodded. "Yeah. Growing the herd."

"Growing hard for Danica, you mean."

Brodie let the rib go this time and instead focused on telling his buddies what his plans were. Somehow it felt a little like betrayal when he hadn't discussed it with Danica earlier. She'd only found out after he'd written her into the story.

Unfair of me. He wouldn't do that again and would apologize next time he saw her. The fact she hadn't said anything about the slight only endeared her more to him. As if he needed it—the moon and stars already hung on her.

"Danica thinks we need to discuss plans soon. I think we need to come up with some ideas between us before we present them to the town. We can't have so many people tossing out ideas or we'll never get anything settled. But we do need to include everyone, and I know Pastor Kent's got some good ideas for bringing people back to Los Vista."

Wydell sat back. "When do you want to do this? Tomorrow night?"

A vision of laying Danica out on a soft mattress and making love to her flitted through his mind. "Soon. I'll get in touch with y'all and we'll discuss ideas." He set his cards in a neat pile. "I'm heading to bed. Getting up at zero dark thirty. Thanks for the game, though. It was like old times."

Almost.

He didn't need to say it. They all heard.

"Go sack out. You need to keep up your energy for that pretty little cowgirl of yours." Garrett's tease followed him out the door, and he flashed them the finger as he went. What they didn't see was his smile.

Chapter Nine

"Fucking hell!" Brodie tossed his pliers into the dirt and stood back to glare at the baler he was working on. One of the parts had bent badly when he'd attempted to pull it from the shed.

"Is there anything I can do?" Danica asked. He looked like a frustrated kid, arms folded, fuming.

"Nothing worse than a broke dick."

Her eyebrows shot upward at that, and he threw her a glance. "Not me. The machine. It's a military term, I guess."

Seeing an opportunity to soothe him, she sidled up to him, an extra sway in her hips. "So you're not having any...trouble?" She covered his fly with her hand and felt it leap beneath her touch.

His eyelids drooped. "Not remotely, darlin'. Not with you around. Where'd you get these shorts?" He ran a fingertip beneath the frayed hem, dipping under the curve of her ass. Liquid heat spread through her core.

Wiggling closer, she knuckled his hat up to see his eyes. "You like my shorts?"

"I love everything about you."

Grinning, she stood on tiptoe for his kiss. The minute their mouths brushed, she felt some of his tension flow away. His crafty fingers continued down and around until he'd reached the point of no return.

She gasped, and he crushed her to him, probing her pussy through the narrow barrier of denim shorts and cotton panties. "Get these shorts off before I tear them off. Then get up on the tractor seat."

Surprise zipped through her. "On the seat?"

"Every rancher's fantasy. Walking in to find a gorgeous woman nekkid on his tractor. Now obey me."

"Or what?"

His dark gaze sent sharp pangs of desire through her system. "Or I'll spank your ass."

Oh God. Now she was never going to obey. She danced backward out of his reach.

When he saw she had no intention of heeding his command, he stalked toward her. With each stride, her need ratcheted higher. He lunged, fingers just grazing her wrist before she jumped out of the way.

"Danica." His solemn tone was a match to dry kindling. She went up in flames.

"No, don't spank me."

"That's exactly what you need, you little wench. Now get your round ass over here and drop your shorts." Before she could think, he moved like a shot. Snatching her around the waist, delivering a hard slap to her backside that resounded with promise.

She panted and her knees threatened to buckle.

"Get these shorts down. Now."

There was no denying him this time. She stripped them down her hips and they fell to her boots.

"Step out of them."

She did, quivering in delight and a measure of apprehension.

His gaze dipped over her pussy and legs. The bulge in his jeans was evident. He sat on a nearby bale and shifted his cock with some effort. Then he patted his knee. "Right here, darlin'."

She gasped. "Bend over your lap?"

"Lay across my knees."

"I-I thought you wanted me on the tractor."

"Changed my mind. You know you want this. If you're good I'll finger your pussy between swats."

Jesus, Mary, and the Holy Ghost.

She had no recollection of moving until her body was supported on warm, strong thighs. A tenderness washed through her heart at the contact she craved. Somehow being in this position wasn't remotely embarrassing or degrading—it was hot as hell. And she felt closer to him than ever.

"Do you trust me, Danica?" He smoothed his hand over her ass cheek, sounding strangled.

"Y-yes."

"Good. You should." He slapped her. She cried out at the skin-on-skin contact and twisted to see his face. She hardly glimpsed the fever in his eyes before he pressed her down again and spanked her other cheek.

Two more times on each side had her writhing and slightly pissed off.

Then he eased two fingers into her wet pussy. Her *soaking-wet* pussy. A deep need sliced through her. She pushed back, aching and too hot. He pulsed his fingers into her pussy until she was whimpering and hung limply over his lap.

When he withdrew his fingers and delivered several more sound smacks, she welcomed the sting. He groaned. "Jesus, you like this. I can smell how aroused you are."

His words only heightened the experience. She mewled, and he smacked her right cheek. The skin was already swollen from the kinky touch, and she gritted her teeth. She trusted him to know when to stop. To know how much she could take.

She wasn't disappointed—he thrust his fingers into her pussy. She cried out at the invasion. How many fingers did he have inside her? Visions of his fat cock gliding in and out had her panting.

Just as she got into the rhythm of his finger-fucking, he stopped. A long heartbeat passed while she waited for the next blow on her ass.

None came.

She nuzzled his shin where her face hung.

"Fucking hell, Danica." He flipped her to face upward and caught her in his arms, cradling her as if she were gunpowder. As his mouth crashed over hers, she scrabbled at his clothing. Why was the man always wearing too many garments? She couldn't get his shirt off fast enough. Her nipples hardened as her fingers skimmed warm, steely flesh.

He cupped her ass and in seconds she realized he was lifting her to stand on the bale between his thighs. She pressed her palms on the barn wall behind his head to steady herself. Her folds grew wetter as she discovered his intention.

The instant his scalding tongue met her needy flesh, she cried out. Pressure built inside her as he tongued her clit, painting a zigzagging pattern over it. In the back of her mind she was aware he was doing something with his hands, but his mouth was too good to think long.

Then he closed his lips around her swollen clit and batted it with his tongue. She peaked. Came apart. Shaking against his assault, finding he was holding her again so she didn't topple over.

She'd barely stopped convulsing before he was dragging her down to sit on his cock. She splintered a second time as he sank into her. Juices flooded. She kissed his still-wet lips and gave herself up to her cowboy.

* * * * *

Dragging his fingers through Danica's hair brought him back to reality. All that thick hair belonged to the woman he shouldn't be touching. As if he cared when he was balls-deep in her.

She rode him like a champion cowgirl, her top abandoned, bouncing on his cock in the throes of ecstasy. He couldn't last. Between her ass, glowing red and hot from his spanking, cradled on his groin and her sweet, breathless cries, he didn't last.

With a roar he came. Jerking upward to bury his shaft to the hilt. She held his gaze, and some inner switch seemed to flip between them. Intimacy bound them.

"Brodie!" His mother's call came too shrill, too close.

"Fuck!" Panic crossed Danica's face as she crawled off his cock and started grabbing for their clothes strewn around the barn.

"Brodie, it's lunchtime."

He wanted to laugh but having his mother interfere at the moment he'd been about to speak soft, reassuring words to the woman he'd just fucked silly made him clench his jaw. *Maybe I'm not supposed to say those things.*

He tossed Danica her top, which she pulled on in a blink. She'd just shimmied into her shorts when he tossed the condom and yanked up his jeans. His belt wasn't buckled when his mother entered the barn.

"Oh. Hello, Danica." His mother's voice took on a world of meaning. Or understanding. His mind was too jostled to think clearly.

"I could hear you, Mom."

She gave him that "don't take that tone with me" look that had made him wither as a child. Now he was just annoyed. He hadn't gotten his after-moments with Danica, and dammit she needed them.

He needed them.

Danica was looking at anything but Brodie or his mother. Her cheeks were bright red, which only reminded him of her other set of red cheeks.

"I figured you were ignoring me. You haven't been coming in for lunch," his mother said.

Shit, he felt guilty enough about letting his mother down since he'd come home. She wanted her old son back, but he was gone. As dead as Matt Pope.

"I'm coming in. We're coming in, right, Danica?"

She nodded but didn't meet his eyes.

He looked at his mother. "Be right there, okay?"

"Five minutes and it will be cold." Her tone softened, probably from the prospect of having another body at the table that might actually eat.

"Give us two." Without waiting for his mother's reply, he turned to Danica. As Ma's footsteps retreated, he wrapped his fingers around Danica's forearm and reeled her close.

When a snort left her, he had to draw away to see if she was crying.

Relief coursed through him. No—laughing.

"How horrible," she murmured, burying her face against his chest.

Tenderness spilled over him. He cocooned her in his hold and kissed her cheeks, her nose, her eyelids. "Are you all right?"

"I'm pretty sure she knew what we were doing."

"I don't mean that." He cradled her ass in one palm, and she winced.

"It won't be nice to sit and eat, but I'll do it. For you." Her eyes were bright with that light he couldn't get enough of. He'd run through flames and dodge bullets to see it.

"I don't relish the thought of sitting down with my parents for lunch either. But let's go."

She took a moment to run her hands over her body as if checking to see if she'd missed an article of clothing. She hadn't. She looked as pretty as a cowgirl boot model.

"You're beautiful. We'd better hurry."

Halfway to the house, she asked the question he hadn't been prepared for. And still didn't know the answer to.

"Brodie, why don't you have an appetite?"

They crossed the threshold. His parents were seated at the small table, soup and sandwiches before them. The rich scents of his favorite, cream of chicken with potatoes, made his mouth water. With any luck he could get a few spoonfuls of the wholesome food in before his stomach cramped.

"Sit down, dear," his mother said. Danica did, shooting him a weary smile. The change in atmosphere was quite apparent between barn and house. What was it about being in here with his parents that unsettled him? They didn't deserve to be treated this way, which only filled him with more guilt.

As if he needed more.

"How's the haying, son?" His father seemed to see too deeply. Brodie felt like a teenager again. He felt like opening his wallet and displaying his stash of condoms so his parents knew he was being responsible.

"Go better if the damn hay rake wasn't bent."

His father pursed his lips. "Try a crowbar yet?"

"No, I was about to." *Before I got distracted.*

Beneath the table, Danica's thigh pressed against his. Having her there warmed him as much as his first bite of soup. She moaned at the delicious flavors and gobbled half her bowl. His mother beamed, and he and his father talked about ways to fix the hay rake and how to avoid trouble in future. Before he knew it, Brodie's spoon scraped the bottom of his bowl.

His mother's eyes swam with tears, and Danica's soft smile melted him. He gave her a wink and picked up his sandwich.

* * * * *

Brodie whistled as he forked fresh hay into the horse stalls. His back was to Danica but she kept throwing glances his way, drinking in the lines of his body as he performed physical labor. His Western shirt tightened across his broad shoulders with every move, giving her yummy shivers of lust.

When he turned and met her gaze, his eyebrows crinkled. "You okay, darlin'?"

Yes. No. She opened her mouth to speak but closed it again, having no idea what she was feeling today. Despite a burning love inside her, she was restless. Edgy. For the past hour since waking she'd been trying to figure it out, but she was coming up blank.

He dropped the shovel where he stood and crossed the barn to her. As her gaze latched onto his concerned expression, a bit of her hard outer shell cracked. She tucked her arms around her middle.

"Whoa. You're not all right. What's eating at you? Is it something I did?" He enveloped her in his arms, drawing her head down on his shoulder.

She shook her head. "It's not you." Saying so aloud only solidified the idea in her mind. After sharing a meal with his family there was a new camaraderie between them. It made her feel good — better than good. As if she belonged with him.

"You aren't wearing that expression for nothing, so what is it?" His gloved fingers worked over her hair.

"I think it was seeing your parents yesterday," she said slowly.

He pulled back to search her eyes. "Did they say something to upset you?"

"Not at all. But they were...parents. And mine..." Without warning, tears burst from her.

"Oh darlin'." He crushed her against him while she cried for everything she'd lost in the past few months—her town, Matt, and now her parents.

"I think..." she gulped between words, "...they need a change of scenery. I think they should move away from the land because all it does now is haunt them with Matt's...memory."

He made sweet shushing noises while she emptied her heart of the burden she hadn't realized she was carrying.

"Have you mentioned this to them?"

She shook her head, taking comfort in the soft cotton of his shirt beneath her cheek and the smell of hard work and the man she loved.

"Do you want me to come and talk to them with you?"

It was her turn to draw away. Backhanding her streaming eyes, she said, "I might think this is right for them, but I could be wrong. Their grief's so fresh."

"That's true." His dark eyes glistened with sadness she knew was reflected in her own.

"I can't help but think if that stupid storm hadn't ripped their world out from under them, they'd be holding up better. They might not have lost their ranch, but they lost all their friends and their lives as they knew them."

"I know the feeling. I have my old bedroom but I can't say this doesn't wear on me too."

She studied his face. She hadn't given it much thought how coming home from a war-torn world to one that wasn't in much better shape would affect him and his friends. Not to mention Matt was gone from his life. From all of theirs.

"Maybe I'm feeling a little punchy today."

He brushed a strand of hair off her cheek, extreme tenderness in his gaze. "What can I do to help?"

Swallowing hard, she parted her lips to speak, expecting to crack a joke about making her scream with pleasure. Instead the furthest thing from her mind popped out. "Will you help me gather everyone for that town meeting we talked about?"

Surprise crossed his handsome features. "Of course, darlin'. I think it's high time."

In one step she was in his arms again, being soothed and babied just the way she needed at that moment. When her tears dried, he handed her his hanky.

"It's clean. I promise I haven't even wiped a bit of horse spit off with it." She sniffled a laugh, and he echoed her smile. "Better now?"

"Yes, thank you, Brodie."

"It's what friends are for."

A sigh burned her chest at his words. They were sleeping together, operating this ranch like a married couple, yet he only considered her a friend? She blew her nose, stuffed the hanky in her pocket, and took up her chores again. Brodie gave her a long, evaluating look before returning to his stall.

They worked like well-oiled gears all morning. Checking the herd, locating an injured cow, and driving it back to the barn where they could keep a better eye on it. When Danica's stomach began to growl, Brodie laughed and suggested she come back home with him so his mother could hover over her instead of worrying how much was left on his plate.

His cheeks looked less hollow today, and she wondered if he'd gotten a good night's sleep along with his good meal yesterday.

"Okay, just let me go into the house and wash up." She mounted the porch steps and Crow raised his head. Due to his old age, he was still recovering from his injuries, but his spirits were up at least.

"I think you've gotten lazier, Crow." Brodie squatted beside the dog to rub his ears as Danica went inside.

The house was as silent as a tomb, and she checked the living room to see her parents staring at a rerun. Heart sinking, she said, "Can I fix you guys some lunch?"

Her mother waved a hand, her eyes void. "I'll make sandwiches in a few."

"Dad? Do you need anything?"

"No, sweetheart. I'll eat later."

Danica studied the man who looked so much like Matt. In her brother's older years he might have looked exactly like this. Held-back tears scalded her nose. They all had some healing to do, but she felt on track with her belief her parents needed a change of scenery or a goal in life. Maybe a new role in the community, rebuilding in the same way organizations like Habitat for Humanity worked.

Her mind latched on to the idea of a community effort to rebuild. As she washed her hands and splashed water on her face, she adopted and rejected ideas. When she met Brodie on the porch and put her hand in his, she felt a lift in spirits.

"What do you think we should discuss at the town meeting?" she asked.

They descended the steps to the grass. Crow didn't bother getting up from his comfy floorboards.

Brodie swung her hand lightly back and forth as they walked. Across the field it would only take them a few minutes to reach his house and a home-cooked meal with real conversation.

"I don't rightly know. The guys and I agreed to talk before the meeting and come up with some ideas to lead them. But now I think we need to gather the input of the town first."

She nodded. "There's no doubt we need businesses to return, and that will bring people. Los Vista is a dead zone."

One glance at his face and she realized her mistake—the military term had probably sent him spiraling into his past. Maybe into the moment of Matt's death.

She reached across her body and squeezed his arm. "I'm sorry."

Startled, he glanced at her. "For what?"

Not knowing if she should go on, she pressed her lips together.

"If you think you have to guard your words for fear of sending me into a PTSD fit, you're mistaken. A lot of things have been triggering bad memories, but not you. Never you."

Damn, their day was carrying more weight than ever. Worries seemed to be piling up.

"Just tell me if I ever say or do something to bother you, Brodie."

"I will, darlin'."

They walked, boots chafing the hay they'd managed to cut in one afternoon. Brodie said after the grass dried for a day or so they'd bale it. Some would be reserved for winter and the rest sold. They also discussed selling a couple middle-aged cows that were good for steaks but not calving.

By the time they reached the Bells' place, they were back on an even keel. Sitting with Brodie's family around the table lifted her spirits even further. When she asked Mrs. Bell what she thought would bring people home to Los Vista, the woman didn't hesitate.

"The church."

Danica blinked and shot Brodie a questioning glance.

"People will travel to worship, and they loved Pastor Kent. We had a real feeling of community. After Sunday services, we'd meet for picnics or in the coffee shop or restaurants around town. If people return for church, even for a few hours, they might remember why they loved living here."

His pa gave a nod of agreement.

"Why hasn't it been rebuilt with insurance money?" Brodie asked around a bite of pork chop.

"From what I hear, Pastor Kent gave all his insurance money away to families in need after the storm," his mother said.

Danica must have had her head in a hole for the past couple months. She hadn't heard, but it was something the man would do, even if it meant he and his family were living in tents. At least the kids had a place to play now.

"So that's number one on our agenda at the town meeting," Danica said with excitement. "We ask for a collection that will go toward building a church."

His mother's smile was infectious. "Yes, that would go far in a feeling of community. You say there's a town meeting?"

"Brodie and his friends and I are trying to pull the town together. We've lost so much but it's time to sprout from the earth and rebuild. It's time to take back our lives." The conviction in her voice seemed to sink into everyone. They stared at her.

Especially Brodie, whose eyes shone with the two things that had uplifted her from the start—affection and admiration. It wasn't love, but she hoped soon he realized how good they were together. She couldn't imagine her life without him now.

* * * * *

From across the room, Brodie watched Danica interact with his friends. He couldn't help but be on edge, seeing her lay a hand on Garrett's arm or laugh at Wydell's joke. His buddies were pigs through and through, and he wouldn't put it past one of them to hit on her.

Or grab her.

If they do, they'll have broken fingers.

His barn had been set up with table and chairs, but nobody was sitting. The guys were flocked around Danica like bees to a flower. She smoothed her hair over her shoulder, where it lay gleaming in rich waves. Brodie bit off a growl. He probably wasn't the only male noticing.

He approached slowly as he'd near an explosive. Danica spoke animatedly with Wydell.

"How did you get such a deep drawl?" she was asking. "It's got more twang than any of ours."

He tipped his hat flirtatiously. "I take that as a compliment. What's a cowboy without some twang?"

She laughed, and Brodie couldn't stand there another second. He reached between the guys' bodies and settled a proprietary hand on Danica's hip. Her gaze latched onto him immediately.

"Excuse me," she said and scooted from the ring of men.

Brodie glanced from face to face. "Let's start this meeting."

Once they'd all taken positions around the table, Garrett reached out and tugged Danica's hair. She batted his hand away but grinned in a way that made Brodie's heart surge.

"Looking good today, Squirt," Garrett drawled.

"Not lookin' too shabby yourself, soldier. Is that a new hat? It's not ratty enough to have been on your head through war." She leaned closer to him, and Brodie clenched his fingers.

"We forgot the beer. Danica, would you mind going into the house for some?" Brodie was being an ass sending her on the errand, but his self-serving side dominated. He didn't want her within a country mile of his friends.

Giving him a funny look, she got up and left the barn to fetch the beer.

"Let's talk about what took place at the town meeting," Brodie opened. Every resident of Los Vista had gathered at the Kents' place to discuss how to fix their town. A young woman who was living in the neighboring town had even come with a pad and paper to record their meeting.

Many people agreed with his mother's view to resurrect the church first—that the community was centered there. But they heard plenty of other good things, such as a feed store and a cabinet-making shop that would employ many people, and one child in the bunch had been certain that with a good ice cream shop, every resident of Los Vista would return tomorrow.

Smiling at the memory, Brodie looked around the table.

"I agree with the church, but you heard Pastor Kent—there are plenty of ways to worship, and money is better spent on housing than on an expensive steeple," Garrett said.

"Yeah, and I think he's right." Wydell looked up from his fingernail he was picking. The redness around his nail made Brodie realize he wasn't alone in feeling out of sorts with his return to civilian life. They all showed signs of stress.

"What are your ideas, Wydell?" Brodie asked.

The man abandoned his nail and rested against the old wooden chair he sat on. "The land has always been a lure. Hikers and vacationers come to experience the beautiful countryside. We're missing an opportunity."

Brodie templed his fingers just as Danica entered the barn carrying a six-pack and a bag of pretzels. When she sidled up to his side and leaned over him to deposit her goodies in the center of the table, Brodie clenched his hands to keep from hauling her into his lap.

But that was exactly what he wanted to do—to show everyone just who was spending time loving her.

"Just what I like to see—a beautiful woman bearing beer and snacks," Garrett said, and everyone laughed.

Her hair fell in a curtain as she twisted to look at him.

Brodie reacted. He settled a hand over hers, and she directed her attention at him. "Would you mind bringing a bottle of whiskey and some glasses too?"

Something moved behind her eyes. "Sure." Straightening away, her lush hair swinging back to kiss her full breasts, she moved away from the table.

The guys watched her go, and Brodie didn't need to turn to know how damn fine her hips looked when she walked. He bit off a growl and shoved beer at the Neanderthals ogling his woman.

Not my woman. Matt's sister who's off-limits.

He wasn't going to answer the next voice in his head that was asking why she was off-limits when she was so willing. He cracked his beer and they spent several minutes discussing Los Vista's high points for tourists. Trails, hunting, horseback riding.

"So we put a few horses on a plot of land and advertise riding," Garrett offered.

"But where people are going to stay is the real problem. They come to town and drop some cash to ride a horse but they don't spend more. We need fairies to move in overnight and build the town again," Wydell said.

Brodie couldn't deny it would be a relief to wake as if from a fairytale sleep and find their world whole again. He scuffed his hand over his jaw.

"We need some housing. I'm thinking vacation homes." Wydell's idea quieted everyone.

"That's not a bad idea," Brodie said slowly. He was doing mental bookwork, shuffling funds from feed and channeling it into vacation homes. Trouble was, the extra funds from ranch profits wouldn't build half a house. Building was costly.

"I think we need industry that will have people wanting to move in. That gentleman at the town meeting suggested a cabinet shop, but I'm thinking big," Garrett said.

"Like a factory?" Brodie was suddenly very aware of Danica's return to the barn. Every eye in the place was pinned on her. At least she wasn't wearing her shorty shorts today, but she would look sexy as hell in a feed sack.

Unable to stop himself, he threw a look at her over his shoulder. She looked pretty as a picture, for sure.

And pissed.

"Am I not allowed to have any input here?" She slammed the bottle on the table along with a stack of red Solo cups.

"'Course you are, Danica. We want to hear everything you have to say." Garrett pitched his voice low.

Brodie's chest rumbled with a growl he never released. "Will you pour us some shots, Danica?"

Her eyes narrowed, and he knew his mistake a split second before the whiskey bottle was upended right over his crotch. The guys hooted with laughter while the liquid drenched his jeans and boxers.

As the final drops dribbled over his lap, she reached across him, her breast brushing his arm as she did, and grabbed a beer. She popped the top.

"How about a beer chaser?" With that, she tipped the can.

* * * * *

Brodie didn't even move a muscle when she dumped all that alcohol on his lap. No, he sat there and took it because he knew he was guilty of treating her like a waitress instead of a valuable member of their group.

She tossed the empty can into his lap. "Anything else you need, Brodie?"

His chest lifted as he inhaled. When he didn't reply, she spun on her heel and walked out.

She hadn't made it ten strides from the barn before he overtook her. She was hauled against his hard — and wet — body, his mouth at her ear.

"Dammit, I'm sorry, darlin'."

She pushed against his chest to free herself. "What was that all about? Do I really seem too airheaded to contribute to the conversation?"

"Not at all." He made a grab for her, but she danced away and started walking. The moonlight carved everything into unfamiliar angles. She'd played hide and seek in the dark on the Bell ranch many times in her youth, but she couldn't make out anything but Brodie.

"I'm going home."

"No! Wait." He jogged to her side. Wrapped his hand around her arm.

She jerked free. "Why don't you go back in and finish deciding what to do with our town?"

"Darlin', wait."

She continued away from the barn, skirting a farm implement parked alongside a shed.

"Danica." He seized her around the middle and lifted her off her feet. She churned her legs in midair, but he refused to release her. Her spine met a hard wall, and he crowded her from the front, pinning her. No escape.

Her traitorous body reacted to his nearness, and even though his fly was wet, she wanted what was beneath it with everything in her being.

He dropped his forehead to hers, holding her prisoner and installing a choking lump in her throat. Dammit, she loved him even when he was being a chauvinistic ass.

"I'm sorry, Danica. I shouldn't have treated you that way."

"Like a cheap waitress?"

"Yes."

"Then why did you?" She wanted to curl around his body, to embrace him with arms and legs both, but she resisted.

"I was trying to get you out of the barn."

"I know. Why?" Her demand was gritty with anger and frustration. Suddenly she was Matt's little sister, unable to join the game but sent off on some silly errand. When she'd return from the house with whatever she'd been sent to fetch, she'd often find the boys gone.

A quivering breath left Brodie. "I didn't like the guys looking at you. Or you flirting with them."

"Flirt—" The word choked off as shock hit her system. Then defiance. "I wasn't flirting!"

"I know that up here." He tapped his temple with a long fingertip. "But here—" he clenched a fist and lightly rapped his heart, sending a pang of absolute love through her, "—I couldn't think straight."

A noise escaped her, and then he was kissing her, swallowing further noises that weren't remotely protests now. She threw her arms around his neck and jerked him down.

With each violent pass of his tongue over hers, she felt his need mounting.

Half-lifting her, he ground his hips against hers. She didn't even care that he was getting her wet. She wanted him.

"Jesus, I need you." He stared into her eyes for a brief heartbeat before picking her up and carrying her away from the shed and the distant voices of the guys in the barn. Shapes rose in the darkness, and she lost her bearings until his boots hit the steps leading into his house.

"Brodie. We can't go in there."

"Can and will. I'm having you in a bed this time, Danica, so I have something to tie you to."

Hot need seeped between her thighs at his dark words. His house was thankfully quiet—his parents in bed. Good thing because a big ex-Marine carrying a tall woman made a lot of noise.

Bumping his door with a shoulder sent it swinging open. In three strides he pressed her onto his bed. She was shaken by what being in his bed meant for their relationship, but she was distracted by his chiseled back as he closed the door.

When he turned to her, lust speared her along with a frisson of trepidation. Even in the dim light falling through the windows, his expression was stony.

"Strip, Danica."

Heart rolling over, she stared up at him. With quick, economical movements that once again reminded her of him in combat, he removed his shirt.

"I said strip."

She shuddered as goose bumps broke over her too-hot flesh. "You're the one who's wet."

"I know. And you're getting naked because I'm telling you to."

He reached for his belt. She pinched the hem of her top and tugged it up and over her head. He bent to remove his boots. Hers dropped over the side of the bed. When each piece of clothing was peeled away and they both were cloaked only in moonlight, she dragged in a full breath.

Brodie crawled up the bed toward her, big muscles rolling, his cock distended and the head shiny with need. It wasn't until he gripped her wrist and looped something around it that she realized he had a length of rope.

The hemp prickled her skin, but it made her feel more alive than she had in a long time. With a tug, one wrist was knotted to his headboard.

"Put your other up here, Danica."

"But how am I going to touch you?"

"You aren't. Put your hand up here."

She folded her fingers but didn't move.

He hovered over her, hot and hard as hell. She wanted him sinking into her until she forgot her own name. But it was clear he wasn't going to give her that until she did his bidding. Slowly, she raised her hand and let him bind her to the headboard.

Let the games begin.

* * * * *

Brodie stood back. His gaze licked over every exquisite inch of his lover's body. Her skin gleamed in the moonlight trickling through his window. With her arms bound over her head, she arched her back in such a way that her breasts were thrust forward. He followed the path down to her abs and the little hoop in her navel.

His palms itched to touch her all over.

"Spread your legs for me." His voice sounded as though he'd been gulping smoke from the aftermath of an explosion.

Her lashes fluttered down to kiss her cheeks as she let her thighs fall apart. The glistening folds revealed to him dragged a rough groan from him.

He wasn't ready to get inside her. Not yet. He couldn't last if he did.

In a blink he'd made up his mind. He grabbed his jeans off the floor. When he pulled his belt through the loops, it made a whirring sound. Her eyes popped open and her breaths came faster.

"What are you doing with that belt?" she asked raggedly.

He didn't respond, only folded the leather in half and wrapped it in his fist. She tensed as he neared, and he leaned over her to gently kiss her plump mouth. She turned into the caress with a coo, and he knew he had her trust.

Withdrawing, he rested the belt on her navel. Her stomach dipped. Lightly he skimmed her flesh with the leather, up between her breasts. Circling the right then the left, avoiding the nipples where she needed his touch most.

"Brodie…"

"Shhhh." He ran the leather up to her collarbone, across her neck, and down her breasts. Across, zigzagging to her navel. Then lower.

She sucked in sharply as he crested her mound. Her thighs fell apart.

"Good little wench. I don't even need to tell you to spread your legs for me." His cock ached, but he held back, mesmerized by what he was doing to her. As he eased the leather over her swollen clit to her soaking seam, she bucked.

Quickly he passed over her swollen flesh to trail the belt down her inner thigh, her knee, calf, and finally her bare toes. "Darlin', what we're doing here, you just need to tell me no or stop and I will. I want you under my command, but the choice is always yours. Say the word and it ends."

"I want this, Brodie." She sounded strangled. Something warm and bright burst in his chest. He couldn't begin to analyze why he needed her relying on him for her pleasure, but it was fucking hot as hell.

His cock bobbed against his abs as he started back up her body. When he reached her pussy, he gave it several light brushes with the leather. She quivered with tension and lifted her hips to meet his touch.

The leather became an extension of him. With teasing lightness, he moved back up her torso to the point of one nipple then the other. Each beaded into hard, suckable points. Biting off a groan, he watched her face shiver with delight.

Drawing the belt up her throat, he said, "Arch your neck."

She tipped her head back, holding his gaze as he brushed her lips with the leather. She gasped, pupils dilating.

"Lick it. Lick it as you would my cock," he grated out.

The instant her tongue lapped the leather, he nearly blew. Balls clenched, his cock throbbing in time to his rapid heartbeat. Precome formed on the tip and ran down the side of his head.

She swirled her tongue, holding his gaze. With each rotation of her tongue he could see her getting more and more excited. So was he and that couldn't happen. Not yet.

He lifted the belt from her lips. Without warning he gave her nipple a light tap. The tip strained harder and a shudder racked her. Closely watching her face, driven by instinct, he delivered the same stinging caress to the other nipple.

"Brodie, please. I need..." Her chest worked.

He hung over her, gazing into her eyes. "You need what, love?"

Her throat worked. "I need to touch you."

"Oh you will. But not yet. First you're going to give yourself up to me and come."

"Yessss."

He tapped her nipples, right, left. Then brought the leather across her clit. She cried out.

"Can you come this way?"

"Maybe. I'm so worked up."

He unfolded the belt and grasped each end. Gently he rested the narrow strip over her pussy. Gripping one end, he tugged, drawing the leather up and over her clit. A ragged moan escaped her, and the headboard rattled as she pulled against her bonds.

When he reached the end of the belt, he twitched it the other direction. As the leather kissed her slick folds, she quaked.

"You're close." It wasn't a question—he knew.

"Uhhh."

The belt made another trip over her pussy. She jerked, and he knew the heavens were about to rain down on his angel. Tossing the belt away, he covered her pussy with his palm, fingers poised to enter her heat.

"You come when I say you can. Your orgasms—and you—belong to me."

Their gazes clashed. In that minute he knew she'd been his since the minute he walked back onto the Pope Ranch.

"Say you're mine," he rasped.

"Yes, Brodie. All yours."

Holding her stare, he plunged two fingers deep in her soaking channel. Her inner walls squeezed him. Five juicy thrusts and she was raising her hips to meet his hand.

"Not yet, love. You're going to come when I say you can."

A whimper slipped from her. "Please, Brodie."

He withdrew his fingers and spanked her pussy. One hard tap that ripped a muffled cry from her throat—a noise he recognized as total pleasure. He delivered several sound spanks. When she was writhing and soaking wet, he delved his fingers into her pussy again.

A choked noise left her. With a wild jerk of her hips, she came around his fingers. Each contraction rocketed up his arm and settled somewhere around his heart. He watched her face, memorizing the shudders of pleasure that enhanced her beauty.

As she gave a final stuttering breath, he hovered over her, eager to kiss her sweet lips. "I let you have that orgasm, darlin'. The next one's for me."

* * * * *

Danica was unbound, on her hands and knees with the strip of leather between her teeth. Her skin prickled as Brodie circled the bed and positioned himself behind her.

The sight of his thick cock had been tormenting her as much as his demands. Now she was finally going to have him where she wanted him—buried deep.

As his warm, steely body was fitted against hers from behind, he reached around and ran the pad of his thumb over her lips. "If you drop the leather I'll use it on you. Now be a good girl and stay quiet."

In the back of her mind she'd realized where they were—in Brodie's house with his parents sleeping at the opposite end. They probably couldn't hear through the thick farmhouse walls, but still... She'd done her best to muffle her noises, yet warmth settled over her cheeks to think she might not have succeeded. Which was why Brodie was ensuring her silence now.

She nodded.

"Good girl."

He groaned as he grasped her hips…and slid home.

Fighting to keep her lips clasped on the belt, she pushed back to take him to the root. Her tissues were still sensitive from her release. Having him stretch her was making her lose her damn mind.

"You're fucking beautiful," he whispered hotly against her ear as he withdrew to the tip and then plunged in—hard. The leather slipped when she gasped. Having him dominate her in the bedroom wasn't something she'd ever imagined in her life. Now that she'd had a taste, she'd never be able to return to boring vanilla sex that didn't have this depth of feeling. Having her mind and pleasure in Brodie's control heightened her every sensation and emotion.

He twitched his hips, fucking her with a shallow thoroughness that stole her breath, alternating that with a violent pounding that ripped a noise from her. The belt slipped and hit the bed.

"Naughty wench. You'll feel that on your backside later." He covered her mouth with his hand, tilting her head back, and fucked her with wild abandon.

A burning need controlled her. His words replayed in her mind—this orgasm was his, and she was going to give him a good one. Her pussy clamped around his length as he filled her over and over.

"Fuck, you're so tight." His rumble vibrated against her throat. She ran her tongue over his fingers covering her mouth.

He bucked harder. His liquid heat flooded her, sending her overboard. Waves of pleasure slammed her system. She gave him five pulsations…six. And then hung in his hold, limp and humming with satisfaction.

Chapter Ten

"Los Vista is right in the bull's-eye and looks like it will be flattened by this supercell sweeping the southwest. The town's three thousand inhabitants need to brace themselves and get underground."

The news bulletin that had broadcast months ago made Brodie cringe. But Danica fizzed with excitement beside him, holding out her cell for him to see. When she'd burst into the barn looking like a kid who'd won the biggest stuffed prize at the fair, he'd been swept away by her fierce expression of joy.

A reporter came on, smiling into the camera in some city far away from Los Vista. "This storm did indeed wipe out the small town of Los Vista, Texas. Damage was devastating. Entire herds of cattle wiped out in an area where the beef industry is king. Houses, businesses, the school...all gone."

A panoramic view of their flattened town was harder to see. When Brodie had arrived, some of the debris had been already cleared away. Seeing the rubble only tightened his chest further.

Sensing his tension, Danica leaned into his side. "It's okay. Keep watching."

"Most of the survivors were forced to move to neighboring towns and try to piece their lives back together. But a few remain. And over the weekend, we got a peek at how gritty these people are..." she grinned into the camera with pearly whites that must have cost as much as a Ferrari, "...and just how determined they are to get their town back."

Brodie blinked, and it wasn't because he was dazzled by a white smile. "What—" he started, but Danica shushed him. He returned his attention to the small screen and listened with wonder as the reporter recounted everything that was discussed at their town meeting.

"That young girl at the meeting is a reporter?" he asked, meeting Danica's bright, excited eyes.

"Yes! Listen!"

The camera flashed to a mail cart. He shook his head. "Wait. Are you telling me that the media has spread our story and people are actually sending donations to help rebuild?"

She bounced up and down like a five-year-old. "It's exactly what's happening! Brodie, there's money. We can have our town back!"

He caught her as she threw herself against his chest. His throat burned with emotion, and not only at the world's goodhearted willingness to help people they didn't know — but because until this minute he hadn't realized how badly Danica needed this too.

As much as he did—maybe more. He squeezed her and lifted her off her feet. She squealed when her hat tumbled off. He stared at her happy face and couldn't resist—he kissed her soundly.

Before he could deepen the kiss, she bounced out of his arms and started talking with her hands. "What should we do with the money? I know the town needs to decide, so we'll have another meeting, but we should—"

"Danica, we have no idea what sort of funds we're talking about. It could be a few dollars. Not enough to do much good."

"Anything helps! And we have some money from hay coming, right? We can dump that back into the pot."

Now this idea he'd given some thought to. They wouldn't have much, but there was one thing their money could do.

"You know the old war memorial in the park?"

She stilled. The air between them hung heavy after his words. Slowly, she nodded.

"I was thinking we could get everyone together and get the park back into shape. The old memorial stone is still there—it just needs leveled up. But our hay money could pay for another stone."

Tears leaped into her eyes. She gave a great sniff and plastered her hand over her mouth. For a painful heartbeat he feared he'd made the wrong choice. Then she nodded vigorously.

"Yes, Brodie. Yes, that would be perfect. For everyone." She threw her arms around his neck and he held her tight, stroking her spine. Yes, for everyone. The Popes would surely benefit from having a special monument to their son.

He kissed Danica's forehead and cradled her face between his hands. "That's what we'll do. Now let's get our cattle fed so we can go into town and share the news."

He looked at her sidelong as she placed her fallen hat back over her dark, shining hair. She looked okay after their kinky sex last night, but was she mentally all right? He'd done things to her that had never come to mind before. Driven by gut instinct to claim her in all ways, he was thoroughly pleased. But was she?

They did barn chores. She went off to feed chickens and cats while he hauled water to one of the pens. Then they met up to saddle their horses and ride out to check the herd.

When he glanced at her proud, straight spine, he saw his Danica. Cowgirl through and through. A woman holding up under the weight of Matt's loss and her parents' grief.

As she rolled in her saddle, realization zapped his heart.

Fuck, he was in love with her.

* * * * *

Danica was nervous as hell about presenting the idea of Matt's memorial to her parents. But she gripped the brochure showcasing a sample photo, drew a deep breath, and walked into the kitchen.

Brodie followed with as much solemnity as he would have following a casket. Danica's heart throbbed in her throat as her parents looked up from the portions of the newspaper they'd split.

"Hey, kiddo. Brodie. Have some coffee." Her father nodded at the empty seats at the table.

Brodie went to the coffeemaker and pulled two mugs from the nearby cupboard. As he poured, Danica settled at the table with her parents.

"That news story is in the Houston paper," her pa said.

She arched a brow. "How did you get a Houston paper?"

"Mail's still gotta come. It's changed hands a few times, but it's plenty readable." As if to demonstrate, her father shook the pages he was holding. When he looked at Danica's face, brackets formed around his mouth.

"Everything all right?"

Her mother's hawk gaze lit on her. Suddenly Brodie set a steaming mug before her, and she was thankful for the distraction. She picked up the mug and sipped the dark brew. In the past few months Brodie had figured out she liked her coffee black. He knew she preferred a certain saddle and how many times it took her to rope an animal.

He also knew just how to make her scream with bliss.

And how far he can push me with his demands.

Beneath her top, her nipples hardened. When he took a seat next to her, she instinctively moved closer to his heat. The action wasn't lost on her parents. Her mother sat up straighter and her pa looked between them.

"You're pregnant," her mother blurted.

Danica blinked. Brodie jerked, and his chair legs scraped the floor. "What? Mom, no. Why would you think that?"

"I can see something is going on between you two. And you're coming to talk to us about something that has lines of worry around your eyes," her mother said.

Shooting a glance at Brodie's face, Danica fought to find words. She didn't have to—Brodie took over.

"It's true Danica and I have been more to each other in the past few weeks, Mrs. Pope." His gaze darted to her pa, but gone were the days when a man needed to ask a father's permission before courting his daughter.

Her father laid the newspaper on the table and filled his empty hands with his mug. "I knew it by looking at you, girl."

Her heart surged and tears pricked at the backs of her eyes. Not only because she was happy that neither parent was protesting Brodie being important to her—but because her father had seen anything but pain and blackness. "You did?"

"Yes, I see you coming in happy and when you look at him…well, it's clear how you feel."

Oh no. She hadn't declared her love to Brodie yet. *Please don't let my father do it first.*

Hurriedly, she said, "Brodie and I didn't want to talk to you about our relationship today. We came to talk about Matt."

The air was sucked from the room. Even Old Crow seemed to wheeze out a breath and fail to take another.

Once more Brodie came to her rescue. Taking the brochure from her hand, he opened it and spread it in the center of the table. "We've got some extra haying money, and we'd like to start this town off right with a new war memorial." With a long, callused finger,

349

he tapped the monument they'd planned to engrave with Sergeant Matthew Pope's name.

Her parents looked at each other and her mom burst into tears. Danica jumped up to circle the table and put her arms around her. "Shh, Mom. I'm sorry to have upset you. I shouldn't have brought it up. We should have waited." The sound of her mother crying wrenched her gut and her own tears began to fall.

Brodie got up too and placed a comforting hand on her spine. "Danica's right. I apologize."

"Nooo," her mother wailed. She lowered her hands to reveal her tear-ravaged face. "These are tears of grief but also of happiness." Her words hiccupped out.

Danica leaned to stare into her mother's eyes, shocked to find a light there instead of just pain or hopelessness. "You…you're happy about this?"

"Yes. It's right to show Matt the respect he deserves. And somehow…this is exactly what I needed today."

Danica reached across the table to take her father's hand. "You feel the same, Pa?"

His jaw worked as he obviously fought his emotion. "Yes, girl. You've done right by Matt and made us proud." He looked between her and Brodie. "Thank you both for this. For working the ranch and trying to breathe for us while our heads have been underwater."

A noise broke from Danica and she squeezed her mom before walking into her daddy's arms. The road ahead of them was a long one, and this was a tiny reprieve from their pain, but she couldn't help but feel they'd made a breakthrough today. Slowly she would get her parents back, and they'd all move forward with their lives.

Maybe someday soon they'd see her married.

When she saw Brodie's shining eyes, she pulled free of her father's embrace and went to him. He held her for a long heartbeat. Did he know she was in love with him? When was the right time to tell him? She feared confessing her feelings would stress him.

She sat down again and her momma got up to bring a pan of blueberry streusel to the table. As she passed slices to all and refilled coffee mugs, they discussed their plans to make the park beautiful and erect the war memorial there. That talk turned to the outpouring of support from neighboring towns and all over the country. People really wanted to help Los Vista residents, and the money was much appreciated.

While they talked, Danica kept stealing glances at her lover. He was looking better lately. Good food and sleep worked wonders on the male species. She couldn't be more relieved to know he was less stressed. The way he spoke and moved ignited her even as she was awestruck by his ideas and understanding of what the town required. What the people needed.

And what I need. He fulfilled her in countless ways. Best friend, amazing lover, business partner. Family. She had to tell him all that was in her heart, and she wasn't going to wait much longer. He deserved to know.

Deep down she held a candle of hope that he'd return the words.

* * * * *

"Things are really coming along here, boys." Mrs. Kent looked around the town. The baby in her arms squirmed, and she adjusted her on her hip.

Brodie couldn't stop his smile from spreading. Since coming home, his friends had cleared a lot of lots. It was amazing how much a team of three was able to achieve. And Team

Danica/Brodie was killing it on the ranch. They had three pregnant cows, and in a few weeks they'd know if there were more.

Besides a cleaner-looking town, the Kent children had a new playground *and* a park to play games in. The war memorial had been set in place a few days before, and the American flag flew high. Flowers were strewn before it, and he knew the Popes were responsible for many of them. Matt's father had given a touching speech about the sacrifices of a family that had nearly brought Brodie to tears.

But he'd pursed his lips and saluted through his choking need to bawl like a baby. Now when he glanced at the memorial, he felt a new inner peace.

Wydell tipped his hat at Mrs. Kent. "Glad to see a good place for your kids to play and grow up. Now if we can talk about getting your husband that church—"

She held up a hand to stop him. Pastor Kent emerged from one of the tents. "What's

354

this I hear about a church? I thought we'd talked about this at the last town meeting. There are plenty of people who need more help than we do." He gathered his wife under his arm, and she leaned against him. "We're doing just fine, aren't we, sweetheart?"

"Yes, we have all we need. What I'd like to see is a place for the Handlers. They could use better living arrangements. I fear that old house they're living in is going to cave in on their heads."

"We're going to check that out today actually," Wydell said. "The bank gave us a statement and there's enough to fix their foundation or maybe even provide them with a new trailer to live in."

Brodie watched his friend take control. That old saying that you didn't really know a person until you'd spent time in a foxhole with him didn't apply here. Brodie didn't know all of Wydell's sides until they'd returned to find their town crushed.

They were elevating it from the ashes, and Wydell's spirit was infectious.

"Oh yes, please let us know the state of the Handlers' home. Then at the next town meeting we can all vote to have the funds given to them." The baby tugged Mrs. Kent's blonde hair.

"Done here," Garrett said as he tossed his shovel into the back of a truck they'd managed to find abandoned and get running. The old Ford was knocking, and it was only a matter of time before all of them were out of a set of wheels.

When asked where they'd found the key to start it, Garrett had given Brodie an evil smile and declared he was good at filing a shank of metal to fit. The Marines had made them resourceful. That and growing up country boys.

"I got the beer chillin'," Boyd called through his cupped hands. They all laughed.

"Go and have your fun," Pastor Kent said.

"Sure you don't want to join us?"

He grinned. "Maybe I'll take you up on that next time. But not tonight."

Garrett fired up the truck with Boyd in shotgun. He squealed tires on the dead main street and whipped the vehicle around to a halt ten feet from Wydell and Brodie. With a whoop, Wydell ran to the truck and launched himself into the bed.

Brodie chuckled at his friends' antics. He tipped his hat to the Kents. One of the children ran up to give him a high-five. "I'll come along for beer."

His mother gasped, and his father roared. Brodie ruffled the boy's hair. "That's a deal — in about fifteen years. I'll still be here."

"Me too!"

Smiling, Brodie walked to the truck, hitched a boot on the bumper, and swung his leg over the tailgate. When he was barely seated, Garrett shot off, zooming through the empty town in a way Brodie hoped wouldn't happen forever. He missed stopping at the few stoplights or for kids crossing the street.

As they bumped out of town and onto a rambling country road, Brodie scanned the world around him. Beautiful couldn't begin to describe the landscape. When he twisted his head, he could see a portion of the fence he and Danica had worked so hard on.

His heart gave a tiny squeeze. After telling her that he and the guys were having a beer-and-cards night, he'd feared her reaction. He'd slyly moved her coffee mug away from her, not wanting his crotch doused with hot liquid.

But she'd leaned to kiss his cheek with a raspy, "Enjoy yourself."

Things had gone from zero to eighty when he threaded his fingers in her hair and held her mouth to his. After that, she'd glided into his lap and moved her hips like a private dancer, which led to her sliding down his body and kneeling before him.

He shuddered at the memory of her sweet mouth wrapped around his cock.

The land rolled, the tips of the grasses glowing gold in the sinking sun. In the distance, a dirt road arched over a hillside that led down to the cave. Maybe he could take Danica there soon. She deserved much more fun than she got.

In the past few days things had really settled in her life. Her parents weren't whole again by any means, but they had sparks of interest in life around them. Over time, they'd recover. And his parents adored her. A meal didn't pass that his mother didn't ask where Danica was. He ate better with her around. Slept better too. She was a good distraction.

The truck sputtered, and a God-awful grinding noise came from the engine. Brodie and Wydell exchanged a look of concern. When the truck jerked as the engine cut out completely, they were able to hear the argument coming from inside.

"Didn't check the oil —"

"Are you kidding me? It's been my damn job to check oil in trucks and machinery the past four years. It's the first thing I checked."

"This hunka junk isn't any better than the Ford. At least she was running."

Boyd and Garrett volleyed with each other a few more times before Garrett tried to start the truck again. The engine did nothing.

Exchanging a pointed look with Wydell, Brodie swung his leg over the tailgate. He dropped to the ground, and Wydell followed. Sticking his head in the passenger's window, he said, "Put 'er in neutral."

Garrett's expression was resigned as he did. Then Wydell and Brodie pushed the truck off to the side of the road. Not that anybody would be coming this direction, but it was the best thing to do.

Slamming the driver's door, Garrett said, "Guess we're walkin', boys."

"No matter," Brodie said, starting off on the mile trek to his ranch. "Weren't we taught to never expect things to go right?"

There were noises of agreement as they headed down the road. As they walked, it was impossible for Brodie to keep some of the ghastly images of war out of his head. But the more he listened to their talk, the more he relaxed.

"This is so much like that camping trip in fourth grade. Remember?" Boyd squashed his hat lower against the fading sun.

Brodie elbowed his friend, and Boyd nudged him back. "Only difference is you don't stink as much. Or maybe you do—I just haven't gotten close enough."

Boyd made a show of sniffing his underarm, which made them all hoot with laughter. "Nobody smelled worse than Matt. That man's feet…" He shuddered.

Brodie barked a laugh. "Yeah, it still haunts me."

Talking of Matt didn't hurt as bad like this. No, this was where Matt belonged—between his best friends. A small smile of happiness spread in Brodie's chest.

The mile passed quickly, but by the time they reached the ranch, he was ready for a cold one. The guys found the card table leaning against the wall and unfolded it. The chairs and barrels were pulled up and the six-pack settled between them.

"Why do I always get this barrel?" Boyd complained.

"You have the most padding on your ass," Garrett replied without looking up from the cards he was dealing.

"What?" Boyd twisted.

"You can't see your own ass, man. Now pick up your cards and stop bitchin'." Garrett grinned at the others then made an exaggerated show of happiness when he looked at his cards.

"Shhiiit, man. We aren't falling for that," Brodie said. "You've got a whole hand of nothing."

Garrett waggled his brows. "I fill my hand pretty well. Plenty of girls' hands too."

Laughter rippled around the table. "Is that so? Where are you finding plenty of girls when you're putting in twelve- to sixteen-hour days on cleanup?" Brodie moved a few cards in his hand, pairing them up.

"Shooters. You may remember a pretty little blonde bartender?" Garrett produced a bag of peanuts, and the guys fell on them like vultures on a roadkill.

"I remember her." Not for the reasons the guys did, though. His memories of that night revolved around a certain tall, sexy brunette with a man she didn't belong with.

That led to him considering his state of mind then. Believing he needed to keep his hands off her for Matt's sake. Somehow along the way she—and her frayed shorts—had wiped the idea straight out of his skull.

As he stared broodingly at his cards, he heard his best buddy's voice.

What are your intentions with my little sis, bro?

I…I don't know. I like her.

Like? That's all you got? She's in love with you, right?

She hasn't said.

Does she need to? It's written all over her and echoes in her every action. Make sure if you're doing it, you're doing right by her.

What's that supposed to mean, Matt?

Women need soft words and gestures. You give her any of those lately? If ever?

Shut up.

"Your play, Pup." Wydell snapped his fingers in front of Brodie's face. He considered his cards, his mind far away. Actually, he was still seeing the wildflowers Wayne had brought for Danica that day. If women liked such gestures, why had she turned away from him as if preferring a dusty truck seat and a trip to the feed store?

He pushed out a sigh.

"He's going to fold. Go on and fold, Brodie," Wydell teased.

"I'm not going to fold." When the words came out, he realized he meant it for all aspects of his life.

He made his play. Banter continued, and this time Wydell was the center of the joke. He took it with his normal good nature, but lines of strain fitted around his mouth. Brodie had seen them plenty of times in the past, especially when they were in the thick of the fighting.

He tossed a peanut at Wydell, striking him in the jaw. It had the desired effect—Wydell's mouth stretched in a grin and he swiped a large hand at Brodie's head. "Why you little pup."

"That's enough, Hard-Ass. You're going to upset the table," Brodie said, ducking the cuffing he was about to receive.

"We're making a run into town tomorrow. You need anything for the ranch, Brodie?" Garrett asked.

They settled back into their card game.

"Nah, Danica and I are good."

That raised a lot of eyebrows around the table—six to be exact. All gazes locked on him.

"So you're good good?" Wydell drawled.

"What the hell's good good?" Brodie kept his voice even. He wasn't ready to explain his relationship with Danica until he'd told her— or figured it out himself.

"We know it's gooooood." Wydell drew an hourglass figure in the air. "But is she your girl?"

"What the hell, are we in sixth grade again?" Talking to his buddies about his feelings for Matt's little sister felt wrong on so many levels. Danica's parents knowing was one thing—they loved her and Matt. But the guys…they worshipped Matt, and his wishes and commands sounded even from the grave.

But maybe Brodie had underestimated his friends. They wanted what was best for him—and Danica.

"When you gonna commit to her, Brodie? She's worth fighting for. Besides, none of us care if you're an old married codger. Just means more beer and women for us."

Brodie shook his head, but the first twinges of a smile tugged at his lips.

"I just wondered because there's talk in town."

He jolted upright, lowering his cards enough that Boyd took a peek at his hand. He laid them flat on the table and glared at each of them. "Tell me what talk."

"It's that teacher again. Wally or—"

"Wayne," he interjected, feeling his muscles tighten with the need to punch something. He didn't like hearing that the guy was talking about her. "What's he saying?"

"I guess he texts her and stuff."

Brodie went dead still. His heart rate slowed as if he were about to take a clean shot. Except his crosshairs weren't on his target — the asshole was miles away.

Part of him realized she was a free woman, able to text whomever she wished. But she was in his life — in his bed. Why talk to Wayne at all?

"Yeah, it's good good," Wydell said, getting a look at whatever was displayed on Brodie's face. "You're in deep, man."

Fuck yeah, he was. But he wasn't about to babble his feelings before Danica even knew. His urge to leave the game and cross the field to Danica burned. No, he wasn't going to act tonight. There was plenty of time to raise the topic tomorrow. They were getting ready for branding.

Talk turned to other topics. He lost every damn hand he played, but his head wasn't in the game either. It was on the Pope Ranch.

Was Danica really texting that asshole? She was alone right now. She might be watching TV with her parents or working on her college courses. But a niggling voice in his head said she could be communicating with Wayne too.

No, she wasn't that type of girl. Besides, she was really into Brodie.

"Uh-oh, guys. Brodie's got that look on his face again."

At Wydell's teasing tone Brodie snapped to attention. "What look?"

"The one you had before you got up and followed Danica out of the barn. After she dumped the beer and whiskey on your crotch."

Hoots of laughter followed, but he ignored them.

"You never did come back, man."

"So?" His voice was raw and carried a bark that sounded like a command.

They guys sat up straighter but nobody was about to heed his warnings now—they were civilians. Friends, not soldiers following him.

"So why don't you just admit to us that you're head over boots for Matt's baby sister?" Wydell's question silenced all.

He looked from face to face. These were his buddies. He'd fought wars with them. Hell, he'd fight wars *for* them. And they'd do the same for him. Time to 'fess up. They all were too damn good at keeping secrets. None of them would slip to Danica before Brodie could tell her how he felt about her.

"All right," he said slowly, "it's true. Things are getting deep with Danica. As if you didn't know."

A couple beers were cracked open, and suddenly Brodie's mouth was parched. He opened a cold one and brought it to his lips.

"Maybe we'd better find this Wayne guy and shut him up."

He lowered his beer. "Why would you shut him up?"

"Well if she's your girl then this guy needs to move on. Right? He shouldn't be telling people they text."

The unspoken words fell between them. *He shouldn't be texting her at all.*

Brodie finished off his beer and sat staring for long minutes while the guys played another hand. He wasn't a jealous type—at least until Danica had sashayed into his life. And goddamn if owning her in the bedroom wasn't spilling into his daily thoughts. She was his, dammit. And he wasn't going to share, not even a few texts.

There was only one thing to do, and it didn't involve hog-tying Wayne and teaching him a lesson — yet.

He needed to confess his feelings to Danica and bind her heart to him. Surely it would be as easy as knotting a rope around her wrists?

Chapter Eleven

Danica hunched over the desk, staring at the books. She'd peered at the numbers until her eyes were crossing, but still she wasn't able to squeeze another drop into the bucket.

She'd run figures several ways—paying this bill or that first. Then ignoring others altogether. Still, she couldn't wring blood from stone, could she? Maybe they should have kept the hay money for the ranch instead of Matt's memorial. Guilt filled her. No, they'd done right by Matt—and her parents. They'd just need to make the money stretch a little further until they started calving and making more.

Frustration tightened the small muscles at her temples, and she rubbed them lightly.

A light tap on the door made her look up. Her gaze scraped over dusty boots and worn jeans, and settled on the belt he'd tormented her with. Her heart flipped. She skimmed her attention over his broad chest covered in a denim shirt. Then settled on his handsome face.

His expression sent a thrill through her. He crossed the room in a few long strides. As he braced a hand on the desk and leaned over her, she tilted her head back for a kiss. The instant their lips brushed, she started to melt.

He broke the kiss too soon, and she felt a mewl of disappointment rise in her throat. His dark eyes burned as he looked down at her. "You're hard at work. I expected you to be outside where cowgirls roam free."

She pushed out a sigh. "Cowgirls might roam free outdoors but ranchers have to look at the books sometimes."

"I can hear in your tone it's not good."

"There's just enough."

"What's the problem then?" He ran a finger over the column of numbers she'd jotted.

"I'm trying to stretch the money."

"Might not be feasible." He tipped his hat back to take a closer look.

"But there's something I want."

The corner of his mouth twitched upward. "What do you want, darlin'?"

Heat trickled low into her belly. "I know somebody who has a pair of miniature longhorns. A good breeding pair."

"Wait — miniature?"

"Yes, they take up less space, which means less erosion of pastures and they're still good beef cattle."

He smiled widely. "You're serious?"

"Well, I thought we could just start with a pair. See if we can breed them and add to a smaller herd. We can put them on the north corner of the ranch. We don't need six-foot fences because they're so short, which is less cost to us."

"Hmm." He leaned over the books and picked up her pencil. Then he nudged her aside. And finally she was pushed so far to the side that her shoulder was crammed against the wall.

Pressing him away enough to stand, she said, "By all means, have a seat, Brodie."

"Oh thanks," he said absently and plopped into the chair she'd vacated. As she rounded the desk, her phone vibrated on the surface.

Brodie snapped to alertness and clapped a hand over her cell, as quick as a venomous snake striking. With her cell trapped beneath his big hand, he dragged it toward him then lifted a hand as if peeking at a coin he'd just flipped.

His face transformed, and she knew exactly what he was looking at—a text from Wayne.

Fucking hell. The guy wouldn't stop, no matter how many times she'd ignored or turned down his offers.

Brodie's shoulders were lumps of granite as he slowly gained his feet and glared at her. "You wanna tell me about this?"

His tone sparked an instant anger inside her. She bit the inside of her lip to keep from spewing it, but he pushed on.

"I heard you've been texting this guy. Why, Danica?"

If his voice had held a hint of hurt, she wouldn't have the urge to lunge across the desk and slap his handsome face. But his voice rang with accusation.

She set her hand on a hip. "Are you saying you don't trust me, Brodie Bell?"

"I'm saying I don't understand why you're spending your days and nights with me, yet you're responding to this guy."

"Who says I'm responding to him?"

"C'mon, Danica. No man's going to keep texting if you're ignoring him. Should I flip back through your messages?"

She gasped. "You wouldn't! What reason do you have to suspect me of cheating on you? Besides, what am I cheating on? Orgasms and dirty words?" Until that minute she hadn't realized how much she needed sweet words. Love words. Angry tears pricked her eyes.

He tossed her phone across the desk and it slid to the floor. "Why don't you reply to your teacher boyfriend? He's waiting."

She swiped her phone off the floor.

"Go on. I'll take care of the books and chores while you make your plans with Wayne."

Hurt mingled with anger. She worked to find words but nothing was anywhere near what she wanted to say. She tightened her lips, on the verge of bursting into tears.

Brodie gave her a cold, hard stare.

She whirled toward the door and then turned back to grab her cell.

"I knew I shouldn't have messed with Matt's little sister."

She stopped dead, heart thumping with the adrenaline in her system. When she shot him a thunderous glare, at least he had the grace to flinch. "I'm sorry you feel that way. At least you don't have to mess with his little sister anymore."

The door slammed behind her.

* * * * *

Seconds after she walked out, Brodie's emotions finally caught up to his mouth. He went to call her back, but the front door slammed. He rushed to the window in time to see her stalking across the yard, long legs carrying her away.

When she climbed into her truck and peeled out of the driveway, his heart ached. After hearing that Wayne was rumored to be texting Danica…then seeing the proof for himself…

He tore off his hat and shoved his fingers into his hair. Dammit. He hadn't meant to lose his cool with her, yet he'd seen red in the blink of an eye. He could still see those words, bright on her screen.

How's my favorite cowgirl?

Brodie's need to pound the man couldn't be realized so he did the only thing he could—he had a mental fight.

She's not your cowgirl. She's mine, goddammit.

Then why's she texting me?

He couldn't answer that question, even in his imagination. He stomped back to the desk and threw himself into the chair. Blankly he stared at the figures for five minutes, ten, before he slammed the book shut and dropped his face into his hands.

Danica wasn't the type of woman to play two men. She must have had a reason for her actions — like being too nice to just give the guy the finger and tell him to get lost.

Brodie gnawed his lip and kneaded his eyes where a dull ache had begun. Matt's voice echoed inside his skull, and he jolted, cracking his knee off the desk hard.

Through a haze of pain, he fought to listen to the words of his best friend, even if they were conjured by his imagination.

I thought you loved her.

I fucking do, man.

So you're going to let her walk out and not go fight for her?

Brodie stood. Sat down again. What the hell was he to do? He didn't have a clue where to find her. If he drove fast, he might be able to catch up with her.

I can call her. Text her too.

No. She'd ignore him. He had visions of her tossing her phone out the window just to escape him. Dammit, he'd hurt her. He'd seen it cross her beautiful features and immediately hated himself.

If he'd driven her into Wayne's arms, he'd never forgive himself. Aching and hollow, he left the Popes' house. Chores weren't something he could ignore, not when animals depended on him.

Unfortunately, he had many hours ahead of him. Working the ranch alone left him miserable. He kept expecting to see Danica at his side, ready to assist with whatever job needed done. But she wasn't there.

He swallowed hard around the lump in his throat. At the far side of the barn her favored mare stomped and brushed the sides of the stall.

Brodie walked up and reached over the door. The horse pushed her nose into his hand for a treat he didn't have. "You miss her, don't you? You need a good gallop. She'll be home soon."

That was one thing he could count on—she wouldn't stay away forever. But the state of their relationship from here on was questionable.

And Wayne could be kissing her right now.

Brodie whirled and slammed the heel of his hand off the nearest barn support post. Dust clogged the air, and Danica's mare snorted in protest. How was it her horse could echo the woman's derisive sounds so easily?

He went to find her an apple and treated the rest of the horses. Then he went out of the barn and started walking through the fields toward the treehouse. His feelings went far beyond partners or even fuck buddies, so why hadn't he told her?

Hours passed while he thrashed himself. The treehouse was too hot to even poke his head in the trapdoor for long, so he sat at the base, picking apart stems and talking to Matt.

If his buddy had gotten a chance at love, he would have grabbed the reins with both hands. He would have grasped the moment and held tight. Brodie had to do the same.

Trouble was, he might have driven Danica away forever.

Finishing evening chores with a deep pain in his heart was no party. He hung around the Popes' place until darkness fell and he had no more excuses. Then he walked home, burning to have Danica back where she belonged—with him.

* * * * *

Danica could hardly move her neck from side to side after spending all night in her truck. She'd slept with her head against the back of the seat but sometime during the wee hours of morning her head had tilted against the window at a bad angle.

Rubbing the sore spot, she groaned. Then her eyes flew open and jerked to her phone on the passenger's seat.

Brodie hadn't contacted her. And thank God Wayne hadn't either. After agreeing to meet him, she realized it was best to let him down face-to-face. He wasn't taking her not-so-subtle hints that she didn't want to date him. Not telling him no in the first place had made a mess of things. Then he'd continued texting and calling, taking her evasion as being too busy to see him, not that she didn't *want* to. Finally, she'd set him straight.

Her actions had gotten her in deep with the man she really wanted. No, needed. But she couldn't be with a man who treated her that way. He'd actually accused her of sleeping with him while sweet-talking Wayne.

Ugh. She sat up straighter and ran her hands through her disheveled hair. When she glanced in the rearview mirror she noted evidence of unhappiness around her lips and eyes. How long before they faded?

She drove across the empty parking lot. Once the lot had been overflowing with faculty cars and even Matt's old Rambler had been parked here. He hadn't been happy about driving his little sister to school, but he had.

Swallowing against tears that rose in her throat at his loss, she considered all she'd gained in the short time since Brodie had returned. Her ranch wasn't in the red even if she didn't have money to buy the pair of miniature longhorns right now. And he'd brought more than ideas to her and the community—he'd brought hope.

God, how was she going to face him again? Working with him day in and out while pretending she wasn't in love with him would be impossible. And avoiding him entirely wouldn't help either of their ranches.

She took her time navigating the back roads home. At each turn memories loomed. As her driveway came into view, she let off the gas. Her truck rolled like a turtle trudging uphill through peanut butter. But she was in no hurry to face Brodie, and he'd surely be in the barn at this time of day.

Steeling herself, she stepped on the gas. She parked her truck haphazardly, jumped out and ran into the house without looking around for the man who'd hurt her. Once she stood in the quiet retreat of her bedroom, she started stripping off her clothes and went into the adjoining bathroom, leaving a trail of stale clothes behind her.

The door exploded inward and bashed off the wall. With a little scream, she ran into her room to see a six-foot tall angry cowboy standing in her bedroom.

His gaze dipped over her mostly bare form and something rippled over his features. "Danica," he grated out.

She settled her hands on her hips, ignoring the pinch of her nipples when his gaze lingered on them. "Get the hell out of my room, Brodie."

"Like hell." He slammed her door shut. She quivered as he took a step toward her.

She threw up her hands to ward him off. "My parents will know you're in here," she whispered.

"They aren't home. They're over at Garrett's place helping out."

Surprise gave her pause. "With what?"

"The guys did some work to clear the broken structure and they're all rebuilding today."

"Really?" She should be there too. Everyone in this town needed help. Wait, what was she thinking? She needed to get Brodie out of her room before he touched her. Then Lord help her, she wouldn't be able to form a coherent thought.

When Brodie got within arms' distance, she put the brakes on. "Look, Brodie, what you said yesterday —"

"Was stupid. I was an asshole, Danica."

No, no, no. This wasn't how things were supposed to go. Her heart was already turning to mush.

"I shouldn't have said those things to you. I don't have any right."

"Exactly, you don't!" Her ire was back in spades.

His voice pitched low with intensity. "I didn't have any right then, because I didn't tell you how I felt. No wonder you viewed our relationship as only sex."

She winced, her heart hammering.

"I never declared my feelings for you."

She wrapped her arms around her bare chest, wishing a hole would open in the floor and she could disappear. She didn't want him to come anywhere close to her heart right now. She was too pissed off.

"Brodie, don't."

He grabbed her waist, swaying her closer. She dug in her heels. "I love you, Danica. I'm so fucking in love with you that I don't know what to do without you."

Her eyelids fluttered at his words. Sweet words—the kind that would play over and over in her mind for the rest of her days. If she decided to forgive him, those words would be shared with her own daughter someday maybe. If they parted, she'd play them on a loop of what might have been.

If he hadn't been a suspicious jerk.

"No, I can't listen to this," she whispered hotly.

"Danica. Darlin', please." His ragged tone threatened to rip away her self-control. She felt herself skidding down a steep slope. But at the bottom, what was there for her?

"Stop. I can't." She shoved past him, too aware of the warm steel of his body. With extreme willpower, she walked to the door and opened it. "Go."

She saw real pain in his eyes. Her heart crushed a bit more. "You really want me to go?"

Dragging in a deep breath, she considered his question. "I'm not the kind of person who jumps to a decision before I've given it a lot of thought. But you hurt me, Brodie. I can't forget that so quickly."

He dropped his hand to his side, where it hung limply. "Is it him then?"

"Are you still beating that dead horse? Dammit, Brodie, I left here and drove straight to Wayne's house, and I told him whatever relationship was between us was all in his head."

He blinked at her. "So you didn't spend the night with him?"

"Hell no. I slept in my truck in the school parking lot. Now get the hell out so I can think."

His throat worked as he swallowed. Then he gave a defeated nod. "All right. You deserve some time." He came toward her, his stare scalding. When he stopped in the doorway, he hovered close, his lips a scant breath away. "This ain't over, darlin'. I'm going to prove to you that I'm the man for you."

Squelching a shiver, she gestured to the door. After she was alone she tucked herself into bed and let her mind work the problem before her. Brodie was in love with her? It explained his jealousy over Wayne. She'd allow him that, but she couldn't get over him throwing her brother up as a barrier between them.

Part of her ached to call him back to her. Another part urged her to let him suffer for a bit longer.

She got up and started the shower. Once steam filled the space, she slipped under the hot spray, dragging in a breath. A sudden noise lifted the hairs all over her body. Seconds later a big male body crowded into the shower with her.

"Brodie, get out!"

He pulled her against him. "I know you love me, you stubborn cowgirl. I'm not leaving until I hear the words."

"Why do you get the words and I had to wait for them?"

"I haven't heard them even one time, dammit. I said them already, but I'll say them a million times if you need to hear them. I love you, Danica Pope. I fell for you the minute I walked back onto this ranch."

Her insides were singing and they'd brought backup dancers, an orchestra, and, hell, a choir. Heart thundering, she stared at his lips, waiting for him to change his story. When he didn't, she couldn't resist cupping his chiseled jaw. She stared into his sincere gaze. "You fell for Matt's little sister? The girl they called Easter who bugged you all the time?"

"That girl is a fond reminder of my childhood. But no, I fell in love with the beautiful woman with enough grit to stand by her parents and try to hold together a ranch." He ran a hand down her slick spine to her backside. She tensed. Brodie had made her anticipate erotic spankings, but he just held her.

Her throat was tight when she finally got the words through them. "I love you, Brodie."

With a growl, he swooped in, flattening her lips beneath his a split second before he swept her mouth with his tongue in wild abandon. She clung to him, water sluicing off their entwined bodies. All the excitement of being in his arms replaced the pain she'd been living with.

As he pressed her to the shower wall, his thick hardness probing her throbbing pussy, he held her gaze. "I want you, darlin'. You belong to me."

"I have for a while now," she said breathlessly. Reaching past him, she grabbed the shampoo. The fruity scents fogged the air as she squirted it directly onto his head. His eyes darkened as she set the bottle down again and plunged her fingers into his hair. Lathering it, massaging his scalp with slow thoroughness.

Once his head was foamy, she ran her hands through the suds on his bulging shoulders, down his back to his carved ass.

A grunt left him. In one of those military-fast moves, he spun her to face the wall. His big body hemmed her in as he fumbled over her head. When the shower spray moved, she gasped. He angled the head right at her pussy.

"Spread your thighs." She did, and he held the water right over the place she needed it most.

Shuddering at the intense feel of warm water massaging her clit, she barely had time to process his words because he scooped her breasts together, cradling them in one big hand. His thumb tweaked one while his long-reaching middle finger flicked her other.

His mouth was hot at her ear. "Feels good, doesn't it, darlin'? You're going to come for me."

"Yesss."

He drew the showerhead closer so the intensity increased on her pussy. She wiggled her ass against his cock, loving the vibration of his chest as he groaned. Biting down on her earlobe, he smoothed his hand down her belly to her pussy. When he parted her lips to give her better access to the water spray, she cried out.

Her entire body was on fire. Her pussy slickened as fast as her natural lubricant washed away. Reaching behind her, she locked her hand on his hip and supported herself against the wall. Legs jelly, a deep ache rising too fast, too sharply.

"Oh God, Brodie." She gulped as her orgasm hit. Sweeping her up in its heated fingers, flipping her until she could barely draw breath.

The intensity of the spray vanished. The drops struck her throbbing flesh from farther away. As it disappeared altogether, he cupped her jaw and drew her face around for his kiss.

"I'm not finished with you," he said, tearing away. Her body pulsated as she realized what she had before her—a beautiful man inside and out.

Water beaded on his shoulders, back, torso. When he twisted to give her a wicked grin, she zeroed in on the water on his tanned cheeks and unshaven jaw.

"Keep looking at me that way and I won't even get you dried off."

"Who needs a towel?" She stepped out of the shower. The curtain swayed behind her.

The water shut off and she heard the scrape of curtain rings along the rod as Brodie stepped out too. Putting extra sashay in her hips, she padded into her bedroom. She went directly to the door and checked the lock. The last thing she needed was her parents walking in on them. Especially this time — it was the first time she'd love Brodie with the words sealing the deal.

When she turned to face him, she found him barely dry too. He'd missed quite a lot of droplets and his dark hair was spiked from the rough toweling he'd given it.

Their gazes caught and held. He held out a hand. She closed the gap and placed her fingers atop his. He enfolded them in his warm, strong grip.

"You're fucking beautiful, Danica. And I'm damn proud to have you."

"Oh Brodie." She wrapped her arms around him. The kiss of bare skin on skin thrilled her right down to her toes. She curled them into the carpet.

"I'm damn lucky too." He nibbled her throat down to her collarbone.

"Mmm. Why's that?"

"I got to the ranch before one of the other guys did. If I hadn't, you would have thrown yourself into his arms."

"Yes, but I wouldn't have held on so long." She stared into his eyes.

His throat worked as he swallowed hard, and then he began to walk her backward to the bed. When her knees struck the mattress, she lowered herself and stretched out, giving him a glimpse he'd remember. Her breasts jiggled and she parted her thighs.

"Stay just like that." He turned away. A blink later his cock was sheathed, standing away from his body like a sword. And he was holding a big pump bottle of her favorite scented lotion.

"What are you doing with that?"

"You'll see." He climbed onto the bed and pumped two dollops into his palm. Then he set aside the lotion and with insane slowness, he rubbed his hands together.

Starting at her ankles, he caressed the lotion into her still-damp skin. Curling his fingers around her bones, making her feel fragile and cherished. He worked upward. Each trace of his finger on the soft underside of her knees sent ripples of pleasure through her whole body.

Then he hit her inner thighs.

She jackknifed, laughter bubbling from her.

He rumbled a laugh. "Ticklish?"

"Yes!"

Still, he wasn't giving up. He splayed her legs and stroked lightly down her inner thighs, painting her with lotion. She giggled hysterically, writhing to get away.

As if he realized his light touches weren't helping ease her fit, he kneaded harder.

She sobered as he ran his hands up to the V of her legs. Firmly trapping her gaze, he slid his hands down each side of her mound. Over her lips to the place where her legs joined her body. Juices flooded her pussy, and she barely bit off a rasping cry.

Carefully avoiding the spot she needed touched most, he continued to work the lotion into her skin. When he reached her nipples, she couldn't hold still another minute. She wrapped her legs around him and yanked him atop her.

His cock crushed against her pussy, and they both fell still. "Little wench, I wasn't finished."

"You'll have a lifetime to finish." Her words roused a smile on his handsome face. The crooked grin made promises she couldn't begin to imagine. Leaning in, he kissed her. Slowly, nibbling and twining his tongue with hers. When her pulse began to pound harder, he caught both her hands in his and pinned them above her head.

With a moan of desire, she did a slow roll beneath him, grinding her pussy against his cock. His foreplay had set the stage. Holding her gaze, he sank into her by degrees, holding her prisoner with his body and hands. She stopped breathing as he stretched her inner walls and gasped when he withdrew.

"Brodie!"

He sank in hard and fast. Withdrew with a maddening slowness before slamming into her pussy again. She hitched her legs around his back, using her heels to try to lever him, but he refused to be rushed.

He rolled his hips like a Chippendale dancer, scraping her deepest spot with his thick cock head. Need bubbled in her veins, threatening to overflow. She jerked her hips into his.

Stealing a kiss again, he slowed the pace. She moaned and he swallowed it. Then he gave a rough plunge that made her cry out. And again. Five more times and she was frantic, reaching toward the bright, hot end only he could give her.

A guttural noise left him. She flashed her gaze to his face to see his features twisted in ecstasy. Knowing he was so close to the edge shot her skyward. With a full-body quake she came. Convulsing around his length, milking him with her inner muscles until she felt him stiffen and the warm jets of his release.

She clung to him as her body played through more than one peak.

* * * * *

Brodie returned to himself slowly, aware first of Danica's warm breaths passing across his neck. He met her gaze, and she smiled. A ray of light in his life. He wasn't ever going to let that glimmer go out.

Rolling to the side, he took her with him. She snuggled with her forehead on his chest and her eyes closed. Which was how he managed to reach over the side of the bed and find what he wanted in his jeans pocket.

When he slipped the humble woven grass ring onto her finger, her eyes flew open and she jerked upright. Her wet hair hung around her beautiful and astonished face. She blinked at the ring.

"Brodie, I never thought you'd remember that grass weaving lesson I'd given you all those years ago."

He studied every nuance of her expression and found she was pleased and slightly pink with excitement. His heart lifted. "You like it?"

She clamped her fingers around it, her eyes flooding with tears. "I love it. I'm going to keep it forever and show our grandbabies."

It was totally perfect for her to say such a thing—he couldn't imagine any other life. "I promise to keep you smiling."

She sniffled. "I promise to support you through all the frustrations of running the Pope-Bell Ranch and fixing our town."

His smile spread. "I promise to take care of you and our families for all our days."

"And I'll learn how to cook."

He chuckled. Turning onto his side, he walked his fingertips up her inner thigh. "I'll own every bit of you."

She pushed him down and stretched atop him. "I look forward to you trying."

He arched a brow. "Trying? You don't know how determined an ex-Marine turned cowboy can be if you think I'll just be trying."

Biting into his lower lip, she giggled. "I love you, Brodie."

He kissed her temple, her eyelids, the tip of her nose, and finally her lips in a lingering caress. When he pulled free, he stared into her warm, happy eyes. "We'll make Matt proud."

She entwined their fingers and curled atop him, right where she belonged.

THE END

Em Petrova

Em Petrova was raised by hippies in the wilds of Pennsylvania but told her parents at the age of four she wanted to be a gypsy when she grew up. She has a soft spot for babies, puppies and 90s Grunge music and believes in Bigfoot and aliens. She started writing at the age of twelve and prides herself on making her characters larger than life and her sex scenes hotter than hot.

She burst into the world of publishing in 2010 after having five beautiful bambinos and figuring they were old enough to get their own snacks while she pounds away at the keys. In her not-so-spare time, she is fur-mommy to a Labradoodle named Daisy Hasselhoff and works as editor with USA Today and New York Times bestselling authors.

Find Em Petrova:

http://empetrova.com

Other Indie Titles by Em Petrova

Blue Collar Dom Series

DIRTY HAIR PULLER

The Boot Knocker Ranch Series

PUSHIN' BUTTONS

BODY LANGUAGE

REINING MEN

ROPIN' HEARTS

ROPE BURN

COWBOY NOT INCLUDED

Country Fever Series

HARD RIDIN'

LIP LOCK

UNBROKEN

SOMETHIN' DIRTY

Rope 'n Ride Series

BUCK

RYDER

RIDGE

WEST

LANE

Rope 'n Ride On Series

JINGLE BOOTS

DOUBLE DIPPIN'

LICKS AND PROMISES

A COWBOY FOR CHRISTMAS

LIPSTICK 'N LEAD

The Dalton Boys

COWBOY CRAZY Hank's story

COWBOY BARGAIN Cash's story

COWBOY CRUSHIN' Witt's story

COWBOY SECRET Beck's story

COWBOY RUSH Kade's Story

Single Titles and Boxes

STRANDED AND STRADDLED

LASSO MY HEART

SINFUL HEARTS

BLOWN DOWN

FALLEN

FEVERED HEARTS

Firehouse 5 Series

ONE FIERY NIGHT

CONTROLLED BURN

SMOLDERING HEARTS

The Quick and the Hot Series

DALLAS NIGHTS

SLICK RIDER

SPURRED ON